JAMIE C☆LLINS

THE
Secrets & Stilettos
SERIES

★

HOT MIC!
Copyright © 2018 by Jamie Collins
All rights reserved.

1793883807

Interior Format by The Killion Group
www.thekilliongroupinc.com

Sign up for the author's New Releases mailing list and get a FREE copy of the novelette, *Sign On!* (The Casting of the Ladies of The Gab – Secrets and Stilettos Prequel).

Go to *www.jamiecollinsauthor.com/free-book-offer* for a FREE copy of *Sign On!*

BOOKS BY
JAMIE COLLINS

★ ★ ★

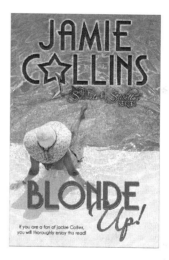

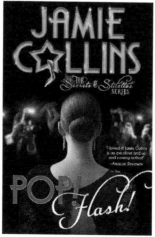

DEDICATION

To my dear friend Sue P.
You are always in my heart.

~ Jamie

PROLOGUE
★ ★ ★

GLOBAL STUDIOS - NEW YORK CITY
AUGUST 21. 2015

JON NOVOTNY, HANNAH'S TRUSTED PRODUCER and colleague circumvented Marney Valentine with a well-timed phone call just as she stepped out of a cab in front of Global Network's executive offices and checked her phone for the hundredth time. There were thirty minutes remaining until the signing of the biggest deal of her client's career to date yet, Hannah was nowhere in sight.

"We've run into a bit of a *situation*," Jon said from the speaker of Marney's smartphone, which was pressed against her multi-pierced earlobe as she headed into the massive lobby and toward the bank of shiny art deco elevators.

"What kind of a situation?" Marney's voice was agitated and about three pitches too high.

"Hannah is going to be delayed—significantly delayed." Jon was cutting in and out and there was commotion that sounded like a battalion on the other end of the line.

"What exactly are you saying, Jon?" The tightness in

Marney's chest was now threatening a full-on panic attack.

"I have called Hannah's lawyer and he will be sitting in for her at the signing. I need for you to arrange for Hannah to conference in. Can you do that, Marney?"

"*What!*" Marney was incredulous. She had just flown in from a hellish layover in Houston on her way back from a three-day bachelorette party on Padre Island with her college gal-pals, and was not in the mood for games, and least of all, for her star client to be MIA. "I suppose I can do that, but is Hannah okay, Jon? Where in the world is she?"

Just then, two plainclothes police officers arrived out of nowhere, flanking her on either side. A third officer positioned himself in front of the revolving glass doors, and thrust a badge in her face.

"Miss Valentine? You are Dr. Hannah Courtland-Murphy's agent, are you not? We'd like to ask you a few questions."

CHAPTER 1

★ ★ ★

CLEVELAND, OHIO
JUNE 20, 2015

PETER STOOD THERE STARCHED, SILENT, and perfect. The initials embossed on his sterling silver cuff links gleamed at the folds of his custom-tailored shirtsleeves. His exquisite silk tie matched his cool blue eyes, and an unusually unstable hand fought to steady a glass of Glenlivet. Pensiveness registered on his face as he considered his wife's words; her back regarding him with cool indifference as she adjusted the hairpins.

"We'll just get through it, okay? It's only a few hours."

He nodded. The movement caused the ice to stir even more. It was agreed, then. One last hoorah, and then the charade would cease. No longer would there be a need to pretend. Not anymore. It was what she wanted. What they both wanted, *right?*

She fastened the pearls, expertly threading the catch behind her neck, like she had done a hundred times before. He caught a glimpse of her décolleté in the mirror. The sight of this simple act reduced him to shame, and he quickly looked away.

They were the pearls that Hannah had worn on their wedding day, that she had borrowed from her mother. Regretfully, the shame overshadowed his sadness that Charlotte Courtland was far too ill to attend the party. Ironically, he would have been spared his mother-in-law's scorn even if she could have come, due to her condition. He had known even back when he married Hannah who he was, and that it was patently wrong to have buried the truth within the sanctity of holy vows.

He was sorry. Sorry beyond words and shrunken by the weight of the whole situation so poignantly that his heart ached in one thousand ways when she turned to him and smiled, in spite of it all.

Hannah—his ever-dutiful wife. Blameless. A woman whom Peter knew greater men than he would give their very souls to adore. He did not need an audience of eight point five million people to tell him so.

"Let's not be late," she said, reaching for her wrap, and then taking her husband's arm. The ride to the reception was quiet. It was better that way. It would take every ounce of strength to keep up appearances, even in the jollity of celebration.

The crowd that began filling the ballroom of the Manchester hours prior had begun spilling out onto the terrace, where additional bars and buffet tables had been stationed. The media held vigil just outside the hotel's massive lobby for hours prior to the first guests' arrival. A media helicopter hovered overhead.

The feel was that of a Hollywood premiere night. It was the largest spectacle the Manchester had hosted in years, where hundreds of adoring fans who felt more like old and trusted friends, had gathered to cheer their beloved

Hannah—true crusader of the everyday hero.

The limo pulled as close to the curb as the driver was able. Security had roped off a clear path from which to escort Hannah and Peter from the car to the ballroom. As they stepped onto lush, red carpet, a sea of flashbulbs exploded from all angles.

The news burned within Hannah to be revealed. It was good, all right. Perfect timing, in fact. Her publicity team said so, and she agreed. She had been advised to wait until tonight, though, to make the big announcement. All would be revealed. Needless to say, her head was spinning.

Why didn't Peter think to give her the same courtesy for the past thirty-eight years? she wondered. His timing was unpropitious, as usual. A boisterous applause greeted them as the couple crossed the ornate threshold to the Grand Ballroom, and Hannah's heart leapt—it was all for her!

The orchestra swelled first with spirited fanfare, and then broke into an unabashedly sultry rendition of "Happy Birthday." Balloons and multicolored confetti flakes floated from the ceiling, filling the enormous room with color.

Hundreds of smiling faces shone adoringly in her direction, whooping and hollering accolades as she made her way through the crowd.

It was quite like a dream. Everyone was present: Friends, family, colleagues. Even many of her long-time listeners from every walk of life. These people *were* her life, and she loved them dearly. Each and every one of them.

"We love you, Hannah!"

"Dr. Hannah—over here!"

Marney Valentine stepped out from behind a cameraman, who was shining a bright yellow light at them, ready to record the moment. The two women embraced gingerly, careful of the beaded dresses, dangling earrings, and lethal lipstick, kissing instead, the perfumed air beside each cheek.

Where Hannah was, Marney ever followed. That was

fact.

Marney was Hannah's unfailing, capable agent with a pixie face and quirky, shockingly orange hair, which fell in a neat ultra-short-cropped bob that resembled a neon helmet. Dramatic feline eyes rimmed with charcoal liner and chic tigerprint spectacles made her look more like a cartoon caricature of herself than herself. Marney's peculiar look was touted *avant-garde* by those in the know, but to Hannah, she was anything but a cartoon; she was a survivor—a product of childhood family dysfunction and a faltering self-esteem who lived a basement-level existence in designer clothes.

Marney had been with Hannah since 2006, before her show went national, when she was languishing in obscurity before the syndication contract, the public appearances, the book signings—and now this once-in-a-lifetime career offer. There was such a thing as loyalty, and Marney well knew the value of it. All the better that it would also serve to advance her own career aspirations. After all, she was thirty-nine years old and not getting any younger.

"Isn't it *fab?*" Marney shouted over the noise, curling her lips and scrunching her nose in just the very way that always made Peter cringe. It was no secret that he flat-out hated her.

Marney grabbed two glasses of champagne from a passing waiter and handed one to Hannah. "C'mon! There's someone I want you to meet."

It was Peter's cue to leave. Disappear. Vaporize. The great cardiac surgeon, Dr. Peter Murphy—no, make that *Mr. Hannah Courtland-Murphy,* was released. Free to go wherever he pleased, his services no longer required. They would take things from here. Hannah's "people" could make careers out of conversations, networking twenty-four/seven. Never tiring. Especially with social affairs like this. These were business events in disguise, even if it was Hannah's sixtieth birthday celebration.

Marney crowded in. "Reuben, may I present Dr. Han-nah—Hannah, this is Reuben Dickerson from Ricon Broadcasting, in Toronto."

Hannah and Reuben shook hands. She feigned for-getfulness when he suggested that they might have met once before, earlier in her career, in Cincinnati at a charity event. He was loath to give her the time of day back then, let alone actually listen to her demo tape. She never forgot a face, especially one as distinctively unattractive as his.

What was it he had told her back then? *Oh, yes.* "*Stick to housewifery, honey. It's more suited to your penchant for nagging rages, which does more to assault the listeners than counsel them.*"

"I'm not sure, perhaps our paths did cross then. It's quite possible." Hannah said.

His smile instantly fell. He caught on and chuckled to himself, allowing her memory to serve as fact. "I'm sure you're right, because if it *was* you back then, I'm positive that I would have been so taken with your infinite charm and talent that I would have signed you up right there on the spot!"

They all laughed at the irony, and Reuben kicked back his cocktail with glee. There was no chance of him making *that* mistake again. He was there to see to it that Han-nah's decision to sign on with his Canadian network was ironclad. He had the contract agreements fifteen floors away, tucked securely in his attaché back up in his hotel room, where a hot little number from the escort service was waiting for him, dressed in scads of black leather and drenching the bed sheets with whipped cream and sticky cherries as they spoke. After the introductions, he would be out of there.

"Then we're all set for 9:00 tomorrow morning?" Reuben said, slapping his pork rind hands together and rubbing them nervously. He appeared to have had enough of Hannah's love-fest and was anxious to get on to one of his own.

"Better make it ten o'clock," Marney said, whisking Hannah off by the arm. "Tonight's party is slated to go all night long, and Hannah does need her rest!"

He waved like a dumb baboon as the two women walked off.

Hannah smiled to herself. Little did Dickerson know that she had no intention of signing anything he had to offer. She was just using Ricon's offer to counter a gargantuan bid to sweeten contract negotiations for the re-signing of *The Dr. Hannah Show* for another five years with Venture Media.

It had been Marney's idea to let Reuben find out like everyone else—at the party that night, when the deal would be announced publicly that Hannah would remain queen of the number one syndicated talk show circuit about to stream nationally on satellite radio. And, as if that weren't enough, fans of the famed psychologist would also learn that they would soon be able to see their favorite radio shrink on TV, as co-anchor and resident problem-solver of the new Global Network's all-women talk show, *The Gab*, an enormous coup d'état in Hannah's skyrocketing career.

Disappointing Reuben Dickerson would be a well-earned pleasure. Hannah felt deeply satisfied at the prospect of being able to stick it to at least one naysayer who had wronged her. Unfortunately, it was the one who mattered least. It was not in Hannah's nature to take pleasure in vengeance, but she had to admit that tonight, it felt good to be taking the spoils of her labors and to be moving on.

The next morning, she finally signed the divorce papers that would end her thirty-eight-year marriage to Peter. All that was left, was for him to sign as well.

CHAPTER 2

★ ★ ★

NEW YORK CITY. NY
(ONE WEEK EARLIER)

THE RADIO STATION WAS DARK, except for the steady glow of amber and white lights emanating from the control room. Adjacent to the studio was a tall glass partition and the ever-present ON-AIR backlit warning light high above the door that connected the two worlds. The only soul present besides the late-night producer was Jeremiah Gaffney, the overnight auditor who was expounding on the virtues of mutual funds and T-bonds to a graveyard-shift engineer.

Hannah waved at them as she passed the plate glass window. It was peaceful. Just the way she liked it. She enjoyed arriving hours before sunrise at four a.m. to prep for her two-hour show. She relished the pre-dawn calm to sip strong brewed coffee and to catch up on reading trade articles, letters from listeners, and not least of all, weekly releases on the rating status of the *The Dr. Hannah Show.*

The halls were empty; the printers silent. There was

nothing to distract her except for her own unsettled thoughts. It had been three months since Peter had completely moved out, and she still thought about him every day. She could not help it.

"You spend nearly twenty-three years with the same man you've called your husband and you forget how to be anything else other than a wife," a listener had lamented just last week on her show. *So true,* Hannah thought, but managed to utter a stern directive instead.

"Then it's time to get to work on the next twenty-three!"

It was all so simple in the framework of two-minute phone conversations. *Real life*—now, that was an entirely different story.

Living life as a free and single woman terrified Hannah. She had been Peter's wife for so long that with his leaving went a significant part of her persona. Even her children, whom she adored more than anything in the world, could not replace the void he had left. Her boys were grown up and gone, but Olivia, her youngest, at just fifteen years old, still needed her. Nothing was going to change the reality that things would be different. Not fame. Not money. Nothing. She would have to ride it out. Advice that she—better than anyone—knew that while easy to dispense, was enormously hard to follow. The most significant work of Hannah's life was about to begin. The sooner that Peter signed on the dotted line, the better.

Dr. Hannah's syndicated hour-long show had aired for only three weeks in 2006 before the first spring book would indicate success or failure. The trends confirmed a positive positioning for The Dr. Hannah Show right out of the gate, which placed her squarely at the helm of the top ten standings for early-morning talk programming now nine years running. She eyed the figures and smiled. The Dr. Hannah Show was currently the company's strongest draw in syndication, ranking number one among women listeners aged 35-64, and number three for women 25-54, which were always prime demographic groups that made advertisers fat and happy. At least something was continuing to go her way.

She opened her designer tote; a homemade card heavy with glitter, macaroni, and Elmer's Glue, had spilled remnants of its design onto her notes and show logs, leaving traces of gold and blue sparkles everywhere. A child's scrawl was written in crayon inside the folded card: WE LOVE YOU, GRANDMA! HUGS AND KISSES X X O O.

She carefully removed the flimsy treasure and placed it proudly on her desk, giving it a place of honor in the gallery of colorfully framed family photographs propped next to her computer.

The twins, Emily and Addison, were five now and proving to be quite a handful for her eldest son, Tyler, and his wife, Sara. Hannah turned on her computer, and it sprang to life with bright white light morphing into a stunning aerial view of a snow-capped mountain diorama glowing in the half-light, stretching across her screen. She clicked onto the multi-colored icon and sent it bouncing. She needed to email the twins their daily comic, just as she did each and every morning. It was from *Farman's Funnies*, a comic series that ran daily both in print and online, which was produced just three floors below the radio station in the company's publishing division. There were indeed perks to being an employee of Venture Media that went beyond the fan mail and accolades—the kind of perks that mattered to five-year-olds in footy pajamas.

The daily comic would be waiting with the subject line filled with emojis and addressed to Tyler on his home office computer, indicating that mail was waiting for the Murphy girls. They awoke each morning in anticipation of just such hope that the comic strip and Grandma's loving message would be there.

Then they would listen to her show, which started at nine a.m. Sara would turn up the sound on her laptop propped up on the kitchen counter while she got their breakfast ready. Together, they would listen with rapt attention to their Grandmother "talk live" on the streaming broadcast.

Hannah placed her fingers on the keyboard and noticed that her hands were shaking. It was all she could do to keep focused as she typed her daily greeting to the girls. Everything was happening so fast. She could fight it—or, embrace it. The choice was hers. But still, she was somehow stuck. The prospect of going it alone terrified her. She took a deep breath. Her heart began to race and her forehead grew warm. She clicked on the send button and closed her eyes. She would never scale the mountains that loomed before her if she refused to let go of the past.

CHAPTER 3
★ ★ ★

VANDERBILT UNIVERSITY
1975

THE FIRST TIME HANNAH HAD ever seen Peter, he was walking with an attractive co-ed across campus. While she found him particularly nice-looking upon first glance, she was not in the practice of stealing other girls' boyfriends, nor dating ones who were smarter than her. Peter was a brilliant scholar. She later discovered that the co-ed was just a friend from his Quantitative Biology class. Hannah and Peter shared the same free period, which was a secluded corner of the library, where they each holed up daily to study. Eventually, they started up a conversation, and that was all it took to spark a fast and exciting romance.

Peter Murphy was the only son of Ingrid and Jamison Murphy, the wealthiest family in Brentwood, which was a small town just outside of Nashville. The Murphys owned several furniture stores across Tennessee. Hannah had transferred to Vanderbilt from Ohio to earn a big-school degree with aspirations of becoming a psychologist, and was avoiding distractions of any kind acclimating to campus life, far from her humble small hometown of Akron. But for the blond-haired boy with the flirty blue eyes, she made every exception. He was a senior—a pre-med student, and one full year ahead of his classmates. He made her feel like a blundering idiot every time she got within fifty feet of him, which was often, as they were inseparable. He adored her spunky, fierce approach to life, her ash-blonde hair, which was cut in a shoulder-length pageboy that swept across her toned shoulders when not pulled off her heart-shaped face with a colorful headband. He loved her smooth, rosy-pink complexion, full, dark brows, and kind, luminous blue eyes that positively sparkled when she laughed. She loved the tall, lanky lacrosse player who, at six-four, towered over her petite five-foot-three-inch frame. He had a boyish grin, scads of wavy, sun-kissed highlights in his auburn hair, and a pronounced Adam's apple that added to his chiseled, European features. His chestnut eyes were playful and warm, matching what she knew to be an old soul behind them.

And so it was, by the year's end, Hannah had found herself talking with the handsome boy who became her regular study partner, and eventually, her boyfriend.

Hannah and Peter dated for six months before they gave in to the throes of passion and finally slept together for the very first time on Hannah's twenty-first birthday. She admired his sense of honor in waiting until she was "ready." It only made her love him all the more. The very next day Peter asked Hannah to be his wife. It was as simple and perfect as that.

The two moved in together and began to immediately plan a wedding for that spring, when Peter would be continuing his graduate studies, much to their parents' collective chagrin. The demands of medical school were grueling, and they were both still so young. Nonetheless, love prevailed, and the two tied the knot in a small roadside chapel that doubled as a recording studio with a neon motorized highway sign that was a saddle that tilted like a bucking bronco. Hannah did her best to make a comfortable home for Peter, although funds were tight and schedules punishing. They decided to take an apartment on campus in order for Peter to be close to his classes and the hospital, enabling him to rest as much as possible between studying and running grueling intern hours at the veterans' hospital.

When able, Peter picked up bartending shifts at a small bar called Lucky's for extra cash. Hannah worked full time as a receptionist at a women's clinic and manned a hotline at a community crisis center in the city most evenings. The newlyweds absolutely refused to take any money from Peter's parents, as there was the issue of pride and self-sufficiency—another notable quality of Peter's sterling character, and just another one of the thousands of things that Hannah loved about him.

It was enough for Peter that his parents funded his tuition and fees, of which, he pledged he would pay back fully once he got his medical practice up and running.

Hannah, two years shy of her Bachelor's degree, opted to put her psychological studies on hold in order to bring in a reliable salary to support the two of them, while Peter continued to study and put in his hours at the hospital. But, by spring, the babies started coming, one by one, assuring with each blue blanket, an end to any hope that Hannah might have had of ever finishing school and getting her own degree—for then.

Together, she and Peter eventually had three sons within a span of eight years. First came Tyler, a quiet, pensive child who made parenthood seem like a breeze, until two years later, when Marc arrived with his booming set of lungs and need for constant attention. Six years passed before the Murphys found that they had been blessed with boy number three—Broderick, with his continuous smile and delightful little giggle that was truly infectious.

Hannah simply loved being a mother. The last-born of three herself, she had never gotten to experience caring for younger siblings growing up. In spite of this, she adored her new role and displayed a fierce maternal instinct that few could match. The family moved to Cuyahoga Falls, Ohio, in the spring of 1988, when the youngest had just turned one. While Broderick was starting to take his fist steps, Peter was making strides with his career, having joined a prestigious team of cardiologists at Cleveland General that ensured a bright future.

Hannah volunteered at the local community center in the city on occasion to assist with the food bank, clothing drives, and, of course, manning the crisis hotline from time to time. This, she could do from home, and really didn't mind the interruptions, as it brought even more purpose to her day, and further enabled her to hone her skills and earn in-field credit hours that would eventually be needed to earn her degree.

Hannah was happy that life had brought her back to Ohio. The fond memories that she had of growing up there, were ones that she'd hoped to impart onto her young family. Whatever the future would bring, she knew they would face it together.

CHAPTER 4
★ ★ ★

CLEVELAND. OHIO
1945

HANNAH'S FATHER, LT. COLONEL ROBERT Courtland, had met Hannah's mother, Charlotte, at a local bar in Cleveland, where Charlotte worked as a dancer. The supper club attracted swing dancers, GIs, and lonely hearts. It was a hide-away appropriately called the Sweet Heart's Club, and on any given night in June, when the troops returned on furlough from distant shores, no red-blooded woman was safe from the tenacious charms of the soldiers who came to Sweet Hearts to dance the night away.

Hannah loved to recount the story of how Robert had been persuaded by his Naval pals to go along one particular evening, and how reluctant he was to do so, as he was pining for a foreign girl whose name, years later, he had forgotten. He had met her in Naples, where his battalion had been stationed. She did not speak a word of English, but managed to hold his fascination for one single afternoon on a shoreline, where he saw her one warm summer day gathering shells along the beach. "I mean to go back someday and marry her," he told his shipmates, who all dissuaded him in jest.

"If you can find her, mate! She's a starfish in the sea. You're dreamin' wide-awake!

"Plenty of American Tootsies to choose from. Jus' look around, why don't cha? Come along with us to the club. We'll show you what you're missin'!"

And so Robert did. Reluctantly, he joined the group and somehow ended up on Mayfield Road, sitting at a table near the stage, drinking expensive wine that was imported from none other than Italy, where they had just served their country with prideful hearts. When the curtain parted and the music came up, there appeared to him, a goddess in the floodlights.

The fourth dancer from the left was a sultry, buxom brunette with mile-high legs and movie star eyes. She moved like magic, and her bright, cheerful smile was positively infectious.

Robert spilled his drink the instant he saw her, never giving mind to the fact that he had completely soaked through the front of his starched Navy-issued whites with crimson wine.

"I was a goner from the get-go," her father would recount, savoring the memory that never lost its power to glaze his eyes over with the image of that incredible night.

Robert had decided then and there that he would have to know the beautiful dancer's name. Embarrassed by the stain, he could not risk her thinking he was off-kilter, so he sent a message backstage scribbled on a matchbook, along with a yellow rose he bought off of the Maître d's lapel on a trade—his ivory-handled sterling pocket knife in exchange for the flower. In Robert Courtland's world, it was well worth the sacrifice, even though the knife was an heirloom of sorts. In the end, it proved to be a very lucky charm, because not twenty minutes later, the beautiful woman emerged from her dressing room with both the rose and the pocketknife in hand.

She had searched the entire club for the patron who asked to make her acquaintance. Bruno, the Maitre d' had shown Lottie, as she was known, the heirloom knife that the sailor had traded for the rose, letting her have it when she asked. "Keep it, *Cherie!*" He smiled. "I was just having some fun with the fellow."

The sentiment touched her so deeply that she just had to meet him herself.

Bruno escorted Lottie to Robert's table, and when their eyes met, all at once, they knew that every tomorrow that was left to be lived would be within each other's embrace.

"*We just knew,*" Hannah's mother would retort. "*The way your heart knows the way home.*"

Hannah loved that story and would yawn copiously as her mother tucked the covers snugly beneath her six-year-old chin. She never tired of hearing it, and often begged her mother to tell it to her over and over, hanging on every word, picturing her parents dancing in the moonlight for hours that night, never wanting to leave each other's side; feeling as if they were floating on air.

When Hannah was older, and later, when she had her own children, she would recant the same story, adding just enough poetic license to the tale until the story began to take on a power and persona that was bigger than life. Like the finest spun fairy tale, the romance of Robert and Charlotte Courtland became family folklore and was, as far as Hannah was concerned, the greatest love story ever told.

CHAPTER 5
★ ★ ★

AKRON. OHIO

THE COURTLANDS WERE STATIONED IN four different cities throughout Roberts's remaining tenure
in the US Navy, until 1966, when he opted to travel no
more and settled his family squarely in the heartland of the
nation in Akron, Ohio, where the family home remained
for the next forty-one years.

Robert Courtland was a master salesman. He sold everything from cutlery to picture books in order to support his
family. "So, what are you *selling*, Hannah Marie?" he would
ask. "Everyone is selling something. It's *who* you are that
makes them want to buy from you. Essentially, then, they
are buying a part of you. Deliver on your word always and
you'll sleep well at night. There's nothing more important
than that."

Hannah did not remember spending much time with
her father during her childhood because he was frequently
away on business. He was not there for picnics or road trips
or tea parties, but she did cherish the times he was able to
spend with her and her siblings. She'd always remember

those wise words, which she would carry with her forever, because Robert Courtland was as good and honest a man as ever there was. His life and what he stood for was gold. She loved him with all her heart.

Charlotte Courtland had continued to work much of her married life, teaching dance classes several nights a week at the city college and at a private studio on weekends. She performed in local theater productions when she could, never stopping her hectic pace, even for the considerations of pregnancy, when, at thirty-eight, she found herself to be expecting a fourth child.

"When is the baby going to be here?" Hannah asked as she helped her mother fold the warm clothes from the Whirlpool dryer and stacked them into neat little piles on top of her father's woodshop table.

"Very soon" Charlotte smiled. "Do you want a little brother, or a little sister?"

"I don't care. Either is fine with me," Hannah said. "I am finally going to be able to be a big sister for once!"

Hannah was the youngest thus far in the family and had two older siblings. Muriel was eighteen and wouldn't be caught dead hanging around her little sister, and JR—Robert Jr., was a very aloof and indifferent fifteen-year-old. Basically, little Hannah had been, up until very soon, on her own in her childhood bubble.

This did not faze Hannah quite as much as her parents might have feared. Hannah was quite content to entertain herself with her games and dolls on her own. There were a few neighborhood children on the same city block whom she played with from time to time, but for the most part, for ten-year-old Hannah, the hours between the end of the school day and suppertime were whiled away in the backyard, riding her shiny Schwinn bicycle, or with her nose in a chapter of a Nancy Drew mystery, propped up against the cherry tree in the backyard, or on her princess pink chiffon bedspread next to her goldfish, Keith's, fish tank.

Being so far in age from her siblings might have proven a problem for a less precocious child than Hannah. Instead, she thrived in the advantages it provided when she found herself more typically than not in the presence of adults, who spoke and laughed and joked with her as if she were not simply an impressionable young girl, but an old soul instead. She was known to have a reputation of scolding her peers for any myriad of childhood mischiefs that she felt transgressed the moral canons of the sisters of the Holy Trinity and her Catholic tutorage. It was not uncommon for her to run in tears to Mother Superior or Monsignor Moriarty whenever she had witnessed the defaming of a textbook, or far worse—a bible. Hannah had little tolerance even then for rule-breakers, even beyond the tenants of the faith. A rule was a rule, and there should be consequences, she portended, for those who broke them. In short, life for young Hannah was very much seen in black or white.

Hannah could even hold her own with her father's stodgy poker buddies, who came to the house once a month to play cards, and who often brought her little gifts like quarters and coloring books. She would greet them at the door with a handshake and a smile. Robert would let her serve them cold bottles of Pabst Blue Ribbon Beer from the fridge, and collect the metal tops as payment. She would then sit on her father's lap until it was her bedtime.

On occasion, Charlotte would take Hannah to work with her at the dance studio, which was once an old garage that had been converted with wooden floors, dance bars, and full-length mirrors. A local businesswoman, Mrs. Ava Kerner, owned the studio. She loved dancing and was once was a prima ballerina herself, as evidenced by the countless black-and-white photos of her looking like a movie star that covered the wood-paneled walls of the studio office. Too old to teach full-time, and further suffering from the limitations of multiple sclerosis, she'd hired Hannah's mother to instruct her clientele—assorted-aged neighborhood children—in the finer points of everything from ballet to jazz.

There was a small room adjacent to the studio, where Mrs. Kerner set up her office, and where Hannah would watch cartoons on a small Panasonic television propped up on a card table, while her mother taught the classes. The Saturday afternoons with Ava Kerner were sublime. She was a frosty old woman with a tightly wound gray chignon, who cussed like a sailor, used a walker, and wielded a yardstick, growling orders to everyone around her—*except* for Hannah. Mrs. Kerner seemed to soften and smile when it was just the two of them sharing a sleeve of Oreos and an episode of *Scooby Doo*. Little was said during those visits, but once the cartoon was over, Mrs. Kerner would shuffle her way back into the studio with her tyrannical summation of the dancers' progress. Everyone feared her booming voice as she tapped the floor with her yardstick and staccato directives, "Point your feet! Butts in! Use your damn brain!" Often she would turn her sour scowl toward Hannah and confide, "It's really not for everyone to find their wings, but the good ones . . . they show themselves *eventually*." She would wink as if it were a secret thing she had just said to Hannah; as if it were one of life's guarded gems of wisdom. And it was.

Unfortunately, in addition to being a talented dance teacher, Charlotte was also a heavy smoker. In spite of this, Robert was loath to make her quit, as she derived, he would say, more pleasure from a single cigarette than anyone he had ever known. Regrettably, just three months later, at the crest of spring, unaware of the repercussions of the toxic effects of the nicotine and carbon monoxide mix on her already high-risk pregnancy, the fourth Courtland baby came prematurely, just shy of seven months—and lived only one day.

CHAPTER 6
★ ★ ★

1965

THE FIRST TIME THAT HANNAH ever saw her father cry changed her life. In the quick second it took to skip down the basement stairs and come upon him, head bent and weeping into his hands, glued her to the floor. He hadn't seen or heard her. The transistor radio perched on the shelf was blaring the Stone's tune "(I Can't Get No) Satisfaction," and the workbench tools dotting the pegboard were vibrating to the three-note guitar riff emanating from the tinny speaker. His massive shoulders were bent over and lifting and falling with his sobbing gasps. This was her hero—a man who could withstand anything. Who never showed fear or weakness, and who could fix everything that was ever broken. The death of baby Grace, as the infant had been named, reduced him to a mere mortal in a single, raw second, when everything that Hannah had thought she knew about being a ten-year-old in an otherwise flawed but bearable world, had changed in an instant. Dreams crumble, heroes fall, and life can rip one's dreams in two. The worst of all evils had come and descended onto her once-pleasant world and took what was right, and beautiful, and true. No amount of prayers would bring her baby sister back or restore her vision of her father as infallible. Ever.

She ran, crying, as fast as she could and as far as her legs would take her, all the way to the overhead pass of the freeway that curved above the pavement at the end of an empty lot a block away from their house. She pounded her fists into the dirt and stones until her pink knuckles bled as she cried into the wind. It was the end of everything that was ever safe and sure in her universe. It was the end of innocence.

The newborn was buried in a cemetery that had a section for young souls. It took an eternity to drive to the cold, grassy landscape dotted with stone markers. First, was an elaborate ceremony that started with what her mother called a *wake*, in which relatives and friends came to view the tiny casket in which her little sister was placed on display in a strange house with several living rooms that were all filled with flowers and people streaming all about and who were speaking in hushed tones. No one really spoke to her or her siblings, who were ushered to the front of the room and told to sit on a worn-down couch that faced the baby's casket. The whole ordeal felt creepy and daunting. Later, there was a Catholic Mass, which Hannah was grateful for, at Immaculate Conception of Mary Church, seeing as how by that time she was sure that it was Jesus who had taken her little sister to heaven, and she was certain it had been for some good reason, even though she could not imagine what that might have been. Giving little Grace back to God seemed like the right thing to do, at least according to her catechism. She knew better than to question what was better left to faith—a faith that now was pointedly shaken and had taken more from them all than just one perfect new life. Still, in that moment, her thoughts were no longer about her own grief. She only cared about her parents and her brother and sister.

What about them, God? she had asked, as she watched her parents cling to one another in the pew, solemn and silent, huddling the family in close as the church bells pealed on that cold, gray day, an eerie and unnerving sound that she would never forget.

It is a sweet notion of belief, as well as a sense of relief, in such a moment when a pure heart receives a *revelation.* It was then clear to Hannah in that instant that her path— her vocation— was decided. She would vow to comfort those in need. This would be her calling.

CHAPTER 7
★ ★ ★

CUYAHOGA FALLS
2003

THE NURSE WOUND THE TINY music box that had been the woman's favorite, hoping that it would soothe her restless thoughts and remind her of a sweeter time, in spite of the storm rolling in from the east and the darkness that fell like a shroud across the window where the snow had begun to fall. No matter. There was a man in a flannel shirt sitting still in the chair across from her. He was tall. He drew long, even breaths. Sitting there, she could tell that he could reach a vase from the tallest shelf or carry in a six-foot pine for the Christmas tree decorating. She liked the way he filled the room with a calm presence. He was vaguely familiar, she thought. Like the pretty melody floating from the bureau.

Then a bluebird landed on her lap, but vanished when she reached to touch it.

CHAPTER 8

★ ★ ★

CLEVELAND, OHIO
2003

"TWO MINUTES TO AIR!" SOMEONE barked.

It was hard for Hannah to believe. An innocent gesture had landed her a guest spot on a major market radio show. It was a listener who had tipped off the morning show producers to Dr. Hannah Courtland-Murphy's unorthodox methods of counseling—and the rest was history.

Two weeks later, she was plunked in the middle of one of the most significant turning points of her entire career.

The show producer, Randy, a stringy-haired twenty-year-old with painful-looking acne and fifty-watt braces on his teeth backed Hannah safely in a spot near a corner desk. "Wait here, please." He wore a black concert T-shirt with cut- off sleeves revealing bony white shoulders and a concave chest. All in all, he looked no older than Marc, her second-born, who was safely studying away at Virginia Tech getting an engineering degree. *Thank God for that,*

Hannah thought uneasily, as she stood glued to the floor in horror.

A few technicians whizzed by, taking no notice of her as she gazed curiously at the peculiar control panel; a labyrinth of blinking lights and twisted cables looking as if it could launch Sputnik into orbit.

I must be crazy to be doing this! she thought, frightfully taking note of the large, glass-walled studio behind her with suspended microphones and equally foreign control panels and equipment looming. A white light box above the steel door, pronounced audaciously in screaming red letters: "ON THE AIR." It glared so threateningly, she could barely breathe.

Through the glass window, she could see them—Kip and Sidney of the famed *Kip & Sidney Morning Show*, seated across from one another, engaged in wildly animated conversation. They were WCLK's morning show team, who took the fine art of bantering to new heights.

On the set, they were fierce rivals, constantly debating opposing views on everything. In real life, they were loving husband and wife. A former lounge show act run out of Vegas for singing too little and talking too much, the duo found their calling in broadcasting. From time to time, the listeners were treated to Kip's commanding mastery of the keyboards and a saucy rendition of a Lionel Richie tune. It was always good for a gag bit.

Kip and Sidney were forty-year-old hippies. Engaging, smart, funny, and entertaining; appealing to audiences from fifteen to fifty, although primarily capturing the middle-aged, intellectual set and homebound housewives, signing on the airwaves at six a.m. on Cleveland's famed "Click Talk-AM."

They started their day at the ungodly hour of two thirty a.m., reviewing newscasts from the prior day, poring over dozens of national newspapers, press releases, rag, entertainment, and trade magazines, and all manner of online gossip and fodder. After finishing their four hour show at ten a.m., they would then eat what would be equivalent to a full course dinner; have a few hours to wind down, then draw the black-out curtains in their bedroom in order to simulate nighttime and "turn in" for the "day" at roughly four p.m.

They would sleep for five hours and then wake to watch the evening newscasts at nine p.m. They ate "breakfast" at ten p.m., while taping the other networks simultaneously on five DVRs set throughout their house.

Sidney enjoyed the quiet midnight hour for meditating and doing Hatha Yoga, while Kip cooked gourmet meals he would freeze and store for the week. Free weekends were a commodity and usually reserved for camping down at Beaver Creek. It was a blissful, twisted existence. And they loved it.

Sidney had received the tip from a listener about a woman in the community nick-named, "Dr. Mom," who volunteered at their local wellness center, counseling wayward teens and battered women in the most unusual way—showing up in a mini-van with a baby in tow! Hannah, back then, was indeed unorthodox in her practice. She was known to follow each and every counseling session with a note of encouragement to the client written on the back of a homemade business card that included her personal phone number and email address if the recipient should need it, with an invitation to "write or call" anytime. Hannah would always include a cookie recipe printed neatly on an index card and a cellophane-wrapped parcel of peanut butter or sugar cookies, stating that nothing helped heal the soul quite like home-baked goodies.

"Find me this woman," Sidney charged, and greasy-haired Randy was on it.

Within two days, he had dug up the "cookie lady's" name

and phone number.

"We'll have her on the show's human interest segment," Sidney had said. "Isn't it darling how she gives all her client's little pink cookie cards? What a hoot! Is she for real?"

The Wellness Center verified that Hannah was indeed in excellent standing as an accredited family care counselor, offering her services—free of charge—one to two times a week. She was especially well-skilled at manning the crisis hotline, and was quite effective with the suicide calls.

A busy mother of three grown boys and now a three-year-old toddler, Hannah still managed, nonetheless, to offer her time and expertise volunteering her services where she felt she could do some good for the community, as she had done after her boys were first born. Hannah still chaired on the hospital fundraiser, maintained the Murphy household affairs, including all finances for her husband's medical practice—all in between baby yoga classes, PTA meetings, and running a home-based counseling practice of her own.

Back in 1995, when her two eldest boys, Ty and Marc, were in high school and Broderick was eight, she had attended night school to pick up the remaining credit hours needed to complete her Bachelor's degree in psychology and family counseling accreditation. Then, in spring of 2000, she earned her doctorate from Ohio State—after having learned that she was pregnant with baby number four just at the beginning of her final year. The news nearly floored her and the family. She had considered the idea of putting the degree on hold, but Peter convinced her to finish out the term. The miracle and surprise of a mid-life pregnancy at a time when Hannah believed her body to be well past its childbearing prime, was a sign of blessings yet to come.

So, she embraced the miracle, and on a sunny day in June, at the quarter hour past noon, while Hannah's entire graduate class was assembled in the auditorium to receive their prestigious doctoral degrees, she was giving birth to

and seven-pound, four-ounce baby girl. She named her
Olivia Grace.

CHAPTER 9
★ ★ ★

CUYAHOGA FALLS
JUNE 2000

HANNAH HELD THE LITTLE PINK bundle, still unable to believe that her body was able to bring such a miraculous wonder into the world. At age forty-five, and with things as they were in her marriage and with both of their hectic schedules and commitments, she'd wondered how on earth it even happened. But, ecstatic she was, beyond words—a sentiment shared by the entire ward at the hospital that viewed the eighteen-hour delivery as nothing short of miraculous. Remarkably, this had been, by far, the easiest child for Hannah to birth, but the labor was a cakewalk compared to the pregnancy.

Her doctor was optimistic yet cautious and had warned Hannah of the potential issues associated with a high-risk pregnancy—high blood pressure, gestational diabetes, and a host of genetic risks, namely having a child with Down syndrome. As potentially expected, Olivia was born at thirty-seven weeks instead of the normal forty-week gestation period, attributed to Hannah's advanced age. Hannah would later laugh that her new little daughter wanted to upstage her mother's graduation by choosing that *exact* day to be born. "She's going to be academic," Hannah said slyly. "It's a sign!"

Luckily, Olivia was a completely healthy and perfect newborn.

Hannah had been so certain that her early signs of pregnancy were that of pending menopause, since she had begun to miss her monthly periods on a semi-regular basis. She even took one home pregnancy test early on that came up negative. Still, she atypically had to use the bathroom constantly, had mood swings, headaches, bouts of nausea, fatigue, and backaches. The day that her OBGYN confirmed the true underlying cause, she nearly fainted.

Getting used to the idea took some time, but Hannah secretly couldn't have been happier. Carrying this incredible secret around and keeping it to herself was one thing, but telling Peter and the boys was going to change everything, so she decided to make it interesting. Just after the first ultrasound had been taken, she arranged to have the family together for dinner and game night. Having everyone together at one time was not an easy feat to pull off. Luckily, it was the Christmas holiday, and the boys were home from their schools. Peter had been evasive all week, as usual, and Hannah was already prepared for the possibility that he might not be able to join them. If so, she would wait until they could all be together. She wanted the element of surprise to be there for everyone equally. Plus, she wanted no chance that Peter would raise concerns. She fully knew the risks and was one hundred percent ready to face them.

After dinner, Hannah had suggested that they play a game of Scrabble. "First, you are all going to get the same set of tiles and will need to rearrange them into a message.

First one to do it is the winner."

She handed the boys and Peter a small felt satchel, each with fourteen tiles. She watched as they laid them out on the table. Broderick scrunched his freckled nose as he spied over at his brother Marc's work. He, too, was struggling with the last part of the phrase. They both had: W-E and A-R-E and P-R-E-G . . ..

Peter stood up, nearly knocking over his chair as the light bulb went off in his brain. "What! Are you serious?" He locked eyes with Hannah, who was smiling. It took her exactly a split second to see that he was not.

"I got it! *We are pregnant!*" Ty announced, late to the game. "Who's pregnant?"

Hannah sheepishly grinned and raised her hand. The boys burst into shouts and laughter.

"Oh my God!" Broderick kept saying over and over, wagging his head. "Is that even *possible?*"

"Apparently so, dickweed," Marc said smacking his little brother in the head. "Yikes! I hope it's a girl. It would be really rad having a baby sister."

"Well, we will see," Hannah said, feeling the cool indifference coming from Peter, who feigned happiness. She knew that it was the last thing in the world he wanted to deal with, and the sentiment simply crushed her heart. "Come on—I made a cake for dessert. Let's celebrate!"

Hannah had long ago decided that she was a one-woman show when it came to her marriage and matters of parenting. Why should this be any different? She would roll with it, just like she had come to do when coping with the curveballs that life was sure to throw at any given moment. The truth being, she could not have been happier to receive what was clearly a miracle.

CHAPTER 10
★ ★ ★

CLEVELAND, OHIO
2003

"YOURS IS QUITE A REMARKABLE story," Sidney greeted as an assistant fitted Hannah's headphones, which kept slipping off her head. A few adjustments rectified the problem. She leaned forward into the microphone that loomed in front of her dauntingly. It was much smaller than Kip and Sidney's microphones, and it did not have a fuzzy foam sock over it, either, like theirs did. She was seated on an uncomfortable high stool that wobbled when she moved. So she tried not to.

The red light over the door meant that they were broadcasting to God knew how many thousands of people at that very moment. It could have been hundreds of thousands for all she knew. The thought of it made her palms sweat. She wondered where the intern went with her purse.

Sidney's voice was sweet and melodic. She was so cool and poised, saying something to Kip that Hannah could not hear. He was scanning a page of copy. They both laughed at something amusing. Hannah was straining to hear through the muffled headphones.

Sidney startled her. "Hannah. What is it they call you again? *Dr. Mom,* is it?"

Hannah nodded, and then quickly jerked forward to respond. "Yes, that's right, Sidney. My eldest son actually coined the phrase. Back then, I had just started my home practice, conducting client sessions with my then-eighteen-month-old not five feet away from me in her playpen. She was an excellent baby, really. Most of my patients said that they didn't mind. For those who did, I had a sitter on call who would watch her there in the house."

Kip commented, somewhat accusatory, "Fascinating. So in between feedings and diaper changes, you repaired troubled marriages. How did you handle feedings? Did you just whip out a boob when the little munchkin got hungry?"

Hannah was cool and took the hit. "No. Actually, I just stuck to helping to repair shattered hearts, broken homes— inflated egos among many other things."

Kip paused, clearly waylaid by the implication.

"That is right," Sidney segued, "Dr. Hannah Courtland-Murphy is a board certified psychotherapist who offers assistance to anyone in matters of family or personal crisis. She's here today to tell us about her work at Cuyahoga Falls Community Center as well as about the other youth crisis centers, in particular right here in Cleveland. We'll be right back to take your calls. So do stay with us. You are listening to *The Kip & Sidney Morning Show* on WCLK-AM."

The "ON THE AIR" light extinguished and Kip kicked his stool. Without so much as a word or nod, he headed for the john. Sidney busied herself with her notes, tossing Hannah a placating smile. "You're doing great, hon. We'll take a few phone calls, chat a little more, and then I'll thank you for stopping by, etc. You can leave once we toss to the news."

The producer hurried by the console, depositing several sheets of copy.

"Use the thirty-second spot on Dawson's Automotive instead of the spaghetti sauce thing, okay? Oh, and Mrs. Murphy, let's try to keep the calls down to one minute each. We're already running a little over. Here we go, folks. This will be ten minutes to the break and then we're out. Keep it lively!"

Kip was not back in the studio when Sidney signed back on. Hannah watched in amazement as the WCLK crew did their jobs. In a symphony of signals and controlled chaos, Sidney was calm and collected.

"Good morning! It's six thirty-five in the city, and this is *The Kip & Sidney Morning Show* on Cleveland's A.M. Talk Leader—WCLK. We're visiting with Dr. Hannah Courtland-Murphy of Cuyahoga Falls, a very unique and unconventional psychotherapist, to say the least whom the locals refer to as, 'Dr. Mom' due to her unorthodox method of treating mental health with TLC. Dr. Courtland Murphy delivers real, honest-to-goodness personalized care to her patients, while toting her young toddler along to sessions. This 'Dr. Mom' has been known to take in wayward teens from time to time, and has even organized a cookie bake-off in her own kitchen, to help families promote the healing process. What exactly is that all about, Doctor?"

"It's simple, really. I present an interesting and somewhat challenging activity for the family unit to partake in together, with the aim that they will bond by creating teamwork through the shared activity. Each individual is given separate parts of a cookie recipe, to encourage them to complete the project of, together, baking a perfect batch of cookies. It's great fun and very interesting to watch. The finished products aren't so bad, either. Most families are truly able to work through the task beautifully. They get 'fooled' into needing one another to achieve the goal. It's often a breakthrough point for all of them. Lots of sugar and tears."

"*Wow*," Sidney said. "That sounds like a great title for your first book—*Sugar and Tears.*"

Hannah smiled, which conveyed as a non-response to the radio listeners.

Sidney laughed at her own little joke and threw it to Kip.

Kip had since returned and was prepared to bite into the topic. "One thinks of a psychologist as an old man with a beard perched behind a large mahogany desk. Not so, I guess, in these modern times."

Hannah relaxed a little, settling into the rhythm of the conversation. But she was not out of the woods yet. She kept imagining an enormous audience of listeners mocking her like Kip had done, or worse yet, waiting for him to make a fool of her again.

"Therapy is not a dirty word," Hannah began. "And it's certainly far more attainable than ever before. Everyone needs some good solid advice from time to time, and a way to sort out what innately, they already know."

"What do you mean by 'already know'?" Kip asked.

"Most of the solutions to our problems are already given to us by way of moral compass, intuition, if you will—we only really need to dig deep to find it. Or, rely on someone to help us see what is in front of us," Hannah said.

"Wow—that is deep stuff, Doc," Kip said, rubbing the stubble on his chin and adjusting his ball cap. "Why don't we see this in action? Care to field a few calls from our listeners? They're dying to talk to you. The phones are buzzing like crazy!"

"I'd love to," Hannah said.

The show concluded after going long, cutting a few minutes into the news, but the producer did not mind. The calls kept streaming in, long after Kip and Sidney signed off for the day, with accolades for the segment. They wanted more—much more—of "Dr. Mom's special brand of healing."

Calls and emails poured in over the next several weeks, asking where they could contact "Dr. Hannah," and when she would be returning to take more calls. In a word, Hannah was a hit. A newfound glory born from less than thirty minutes at a hot mic on a station ranked second among adult listeners ages 25-54. Eastern Ohio was listening.

The station's general manager, Buford Jones, was just getting up for an early-morning pee when he caught the beginning of Hannah's segment on the bathroom radio, which he was in the habit of switching on, first thing, each and every morning. He had the sound system wired so that he was able to access and monitor the station from just about any room of the house. He turned the volume up on a speaker mounted on the bathroom wall and sat butt naked on the edge of the commode—and listened.

"Hi, Dr. Hannah—my name is Sue Ann from Medina. I have a grown kid who won't leave the nest. My son is nearly thirty. He loses every job he gets; he's always broke, and is always borrowing money from us. What can my husband and I do?"

"You can stop making it easy for him!" Hannah's reply was clear. "You and your husband are not an ATM!"

"I suppose you're right . . ." the caller hedged.

"Sue Ann! Wake up—he is a grown man, and by providing an option for him, you are never going to help him feel the *need* to do better. Time's up! Push that bird out of the nest. I assure you, he will fly on his own. Next caller, please."

"Hi, I'm Jason from Cleveland . . . I'm on my second marriage, and I'm having an issue with my ex-wife, who also happens to be my business partner."

"Your *business partner*? What kind of business are you still in with your ex-wife?" Hannah said.

"We own a bar together."

"Yeah, well, Jason, my advice to you would be to extract yourself from that potential minefield. That is, if you want your second marriage to have any chance of surviving. Running a business with a partner is hard enough, without the added drama and history of being former spouses. I urge you to deem *last call* and get all the way out of that arrangement. Do you and your ex have any children?"

"No, Dr. Hannah."

"Good. Get a lawyer and move on to your next business venture, perhaps with your current life-partner!"

Hannah was a *natural*. Buford liked the way she engaged with each caller, building a rapport within the first few seconds, and then diving into the problem at hand. One right after the other—issues with break-ups, finances, health problems, and mid-life crises. Everything from parenting dilemmas to gambling addictions to overeating and compulsive disorders—they just kept coming.

She had polish, was professional and credible. And she had just enough chutzpah to command attention—even if one did not like or agree with the advice she was dispensing. Jones had the sense that she could single-handedly bring a lumberjack to tears. She had to be quick when doling advice, which added to her persona of being a bit hard-nosed. This, he saw as another plus. She was no pushover, that was for sure—and all that would be good for ratings. Radio shrinks with *attitude* were the next big ticket. He followed the trends, and she was the best he had heard to date.

Jones fastened a towel around his enormous gut and reached for his cell phone. He had to call the show manager, Gregg Linden, right away and ask his opinion on the segment. And more importantly, to find out if Hannah was available for hire.

Dorleen, Jones's wife of ten years, observed his frantic dance with amusement—bath towel slipping and all—as he ran around the bedroom, riffling through the bureau, tossing socks and underwear in all directions.

"Where are my favorite drawers, baby? The silk ones?"

"What's the big hurry, sugar? I don't see any fire."

"Gotta find that Dr. Hannah woman and sign her on before someone else beats me to it—that's what!"

Dorleen yawned. "Baby, it's six thirty in the morning. You don't have to be down at the office until nine. Come on back to bed."

She pushed back the covers and stretched languorously, patting his pillow temptingly. Few things mattered as much in life to Buford Jones as making money, but one of them was Dorleen. He hedged.

"Aw, c'mon now, baby. Don't lie there looking so luscious and all. I got a job to do, woman."

His young wife smiled wryly, stretching ever so seductively, letting the lace from her camisole show him just what he was missing.

"Go on, then. I ain't stoppin' you," she teased half-convincingly. Her pouty frown positively did him in.

Buford considered the desk clock, his business suit in hand, and the purring vixen beckoning from his bed. *Damn.* After all, he was not *crazy!*

Tossing the suit aside with a flourish, he let the towel drop to the floor in a heap, and joined her. "Hell, I guess that the mom-shrink can wait just a little bit longer!"

CHAPTER 11
★ ★ ★

AKRON, OHIO
1972

HANNAH'S MIDDLE SCHOOL YEARS HAD been mostly filled with books and the occasional stray dog or cat brought home for Robert and Charlotte to help her care for. There was rarely ever an empty birdcage or hamster wheel in the house that wasn't spinning with some form of rodent living the life of Riley. Hannah most definitely had a soft spot for strays and excelled when giving nurturing love and care to anyone, or anything, who needed her.

In her freshman year, Hannah enrolled at Our Lady of the Elms, an all-girls prep school founded by the Sisters of St. Dominic. By Hannah's sophomore year, she had taken a part-time job at an animal shelter and, in addition to her studies, volunteered at the local Boys and Girls' Club as a youth aide tutoring fifth-graders after school. This is where the counseling bug bit her, as she watched with fascination how the seasoned youth advisers worked so effectively with the young people and families who were in various levels of need in the community. One such volunteer was Scarlett, a tall, spirited co-ed who worked in the sports and recreation program. She was an athlete—a star volleyball player with a desire to bring a love of health and fitness to middle school and high school girls too shy to interact in team sports. She ran jazzercise classes to funky Motown tunes that got the girls dancing and jumping, while lifting their spirits. Scarlett wore shiny leotards, colorful headbands, and legwarmers. She counted out each step like a pro. She had a long blonde braid that cascaded down her back, and she looked like a life-sized Barbie doll. Hannah marveled at the way she could connect with a room of sullen, shy girls, quickly transforming them into a fit of giggles and grins once they started moving.

Feeling blessed and somewhat privileged caused Hannah to want to do more to help others herself. It simply was how she was wired. Everyone had his or her own special style. She was determined to find her own.

While the world around her was watching the demonstrations in Washington DC, against the Vietnam War, lamenting the breakup of The Beatles and following the *Apollo 13* Mission to nowhere, Hannah was working hard at her studies and hoping to maintain a solid grade point average that would get her into Vanderbilt.

High school brought new challenges and with them, opportunities for Hannah to shine both in her studies, as well as her extra-curricular endeavors. She joined every club she could her junior and senior year, including the yearbook committee, so that she could interview fellow students and have a say as to how their precious high school memories would be forever documented in the yearbook annuals for years to come. One of her favorite tasks was interviewing campus celebrities for the articles. That's how she met her best friend, Keira Clark, who was the star vocalist in all of the school plays and all-around most popular girl in the graduating class. Half of the layouts in the yearbook's arts section featured Keira commanding the stage with her stellar voice cast in musicals and headlining talent showcase nights. What Keira lacked in academics, she had in spades in the looks and personality department. A beautiful All-American teen with long brown hair, thoroughbred legs, and a pageant smile, Keira had a penchant for attention—and drama. She had abysmal grades, but sang like an angel, starring in every school production from *Grease* to *Godspell*.

Keira kept her then-new best friend, Hannah, busy policing her every move and rescuing her from disastrous dates, looming deadlines, and bad decisions, more often than not. Hannah didn't mind. She was happy to hang out with her spirited friend and more or less live vicariously through her exploits. The two balanced each other out, as they were so opposite in every way. Hannah was practical and pretty, and Keira was Hannah's ticket into the world of the "popular crowd," even if only by association. The two friends and were thick as thieves all the way through senior year. So, it was no surprise that they decided that they would double date to the prom.

Hannah agreed to go with the first boy who had asked her to accompany him from St. Vincent's, which was the all-boys brother school to Our Land of the Elms. Marty Paige was a quiet type, whom she had known from church and choir from the middle school years, who had emerged from puberty with a deeper voice and a decent car. She had figured that he was a safe bet as a platonic escort that with little incident, would get her home in one piece with fairly pleasant prom-night memories for her journal. Keira, on the other hand, went big with the formidable choice of asking an older boy—and former graduate of the local public school—to accompany her. They would be arriving at the event on the back of his Honda motorcycle.

"We'll meet up there, okay, Hannah?" Keira said at the bus stop, pulling a Winston from her suede-fringed purse, jingling a wristful of Janice Joplin bracelets. She was always so chic and colorful.

"Really?" Hannah said. "I thought the idea was that we were going to go together—as two couples."

"Relax—it will be fine. That way, you will be able to leave when you're ready. I am planning on partying till dawn, and I *know* that's not you're style."

If it had been up to Hannah, she would not even go to the prom. A bag of popcorn and a good movie would have been more her idea of a pleasant Friday night. She had heard that, *What's Up, Doc?* was playing at the Main Street Movie Theater. What was better than Streisand?

"It's gonna be a blast, Hannah. I promise. I'll call you tonight, and we'll go over what we are going to wear, and all that, okay? I gotta catch this bus."

Hannah sighed and smiled. The war might have been ending in Vietnam, but the likes of Miss Keira Clark—and the class of 1972—would soon be unleashed on the world.

Hannah never made it to the prom. She spent most of the evening holding Keira's gorgeous hair back as she hurled into the toilet in the girls' restroom. A Quaalude cocktail compliments of her stoner date rendered Keira nearly comatose not one hour into the festivities. *Such a waste of energy*, Hannah thought as she sat with her friend on the cold tile floor, keeping her opinions to herself. *What would it matter? Hadn't Keira suffered enough already?* The prom would commence without them, floating on the edge of teen angst mixing with the rhythms of Led Zeppelin's haunting, anthem, "Stairway to Heaven" drifting up into the rafters of the gymnasium. Hannah steadied herself for what was going to be a long night.

CHAPTER 12
★ ★ ★

CUYAHOGA FALLS
2003

NIGHTTIME WAS THE HARDEST. LIKE a dream, one day flowed into the next, but then she worried. What about the children? Wouldn't they be missing her and wondering where she'd gone? And what about her own mother? Then, as soon as one nagging thought would arise, another floated in to take its place.

The water boiling on the stove—had she remembered to turn off the flame?

What about the man in the flannel shirt? When would he back? She liked him so. He smelled like cedar chips and musk.

She noticed a shadow on the wall. It flickered like an angel dancing in the moonlight. Now that would do.

And with the humming of its wings, she was lost to sleep.

CHAPTER 13
★ ★ ★

2003

HANNAH WAS KNEE-DEEP IN ALLIGATORS when she got the call. The house was in chaos. With the washing machine being on the fritz, piles of dirty clothes were strewn in a path leading to a larger heap in the center of the laundry room. She stepped over a stray sneaker and bemoaned, "*Seriously?* Broderick—hurry up, or you'll be late for class!"

The high school junior lumbered into the kitchen half-dressed, with car keys in hand. He started poking around for his other shoe. "Do we have any Pop-Tarts?" he asked, riffling through the cabinets above the sink.

"Here is your other shoe—I almost wiped out on it. Why don't you take a banana instead?" Hannah said. "It's better for you."

He grabbed two from the bunch and headed for the door.

"No books?" Hannah said, assessing the contents of his empty backpack.

"They're in the car. I have practice today after school, so I'll grab dinner at the mall," he said, checking his phone that had pinged with a text. He then disappeared through the back door. "Peace—out!"

Hannah didn't waver. "Don't text and drive!" she called to the closed door. He was a thunderstorm of sorts. Always running behind, and cared little for rules or tradition. A typical nearly seventeen-year-old.

She turned her attention to the matter at hand. Olivia was busily stirring up a mess of Cheerios and banana slices on the table from the towering height of her booster chair. Hannah sighed. She still had to start the casserole for the clinic pot luck, then run to the grocery store for more milk with Olivia in tow, who, no doubt would object to being jammed in a car seat when she would rather be enjoying her mid-morning nap on account of the nanny being out sick that morning and causing plans to be altered. Jaden, the backup sitter, would not be available to stay with Olivia while Hannah ran her errands and worked that day in her home office. Instead, Hannah would have to cancel her nine o'clock appointment, and then reschedule her one o'clock session, which she could do from the car, when taking the German Shepherd, Sigmund, to the vet for his flea dip. Peter was planning to attend a medical confer- ence in San Francisco and would be leaving on Saturday. She had forgotten to take his blue suit to the cleaners to be pressed. Now, she would have to find a one-hour dry cleaner at the mall later in the afternoon, somewhere between picking up extra business cards and office supplies for her new mass mailing and getting Olivia and herself to their "Mommy and Me" yoga class by 3:00 p.m. sharp.

Hannah ran her private practice from the den. It was a converted home office in which clients had to use the front entrance of the house to access, but they did not mind. It gave them the subtle feeling of coming to their sessions to see a "friend" rather than a health care professional. It was simply another means by which Hannah was able to provide highly individualized personal care to her regular clients. Oftentimes she would conduct the therapy sessions with Olivia propped contently in her baby swing, or in her playpen. A pot of tea was always standard at one of Dr. Hannah's sessions; a bookshelf of self-help materials were available on loan, and always—those magnificent home-baked cookies were prominently showcased on the coffee table for the taking. Hannah never deviated from her tried and true tactics that seemed to work so well for her clients.

She caught the cordless phone perched on the counter on the first ring, figuring it was Peter, as clients never called on the landline.

"Hello—"

"Good morning. Is this is Dr. Hannah Courtland-Murphy?"

"Yes, it is."

The man's voice was unfamiliar to her.

"I'm glad I was able to catch you. I'm sure your schedule has you hopping, so I'll be brief. My name is Buford Jones, Ms. Murphy. I am the station manager of WCLK-AM. How did you like guest-appearing the other day on Kip and Sidney's show?"

She snapped a sheet of paper towel from the roll to mop up the mess of apple juice that had just toppled over and made its way to the kitchen floor. Olivia started to fuss, her little bottom lip quivering. Hannah lifted her from the seat and propped her astride her hip. She searched the dishwasher for a new lid for the sippy cup.

"Yes, I did, Mr. Jones . . . I enjoyed it very much, thank you. It was great fun."

"Good, then. I'm glad to hear that. So, what do you think about the wonderful world of broadcasting? Pretty intense, huh?"

She laughed agreeably, taking his lead. How nice of him

to call and thank her personally. She did not think that the segment had gone that entirely well, but he did seem happy. In truth, she had found Kip to be a rude, arrogant snob, and she was glad to have the whole ordeal behind her. As far as Sidney, it was Hannah's opinion that Sidney simply had no control with the callers. But what did she know?

"It was a treat, Mr. Jones. I thoroughly enjoyed being grilled. No, seriously, the publicity was great. My phone hasn't stopped ringing," she'd fibbed.

"Oh, that's great. Well, we think you were terrific. The station got a good amount of positive response to the segment, and that, actually, is what I'm calling about. Might you be free for lunch? I'd like to talk to you about some ideas we're kicking around about featuring you again on the show. How do you feel about that?"

"Well, I . . . " Hannah was stunned. *Did he just say what I think he just said? What does he mean by 'feature you again'?* She hesitated.

"I'm sure you're busy, so I promise, I won't take more than an hour of your time. How about, say, eleven forty-five at Louigi's?" Buford said.

Today? Hannah panicked. Olivia was squirming out of her arms, wanting to be put down and bracing herself for a blood-curdling scream.

Hannah hurried Jones off with what he most wanted to hear, and what she *least* wanted to say.

"Okay, great . . . I'll see you there. Bye."

Olivia hauled off and wailed just as Hannah hung up the receiver, giant tears springing in her eyes as she rubbed her leaky nose. Hannah shook her head and sighed, defeated.

"You and me both, baby."

The restaurant was inconveniently located in the heart

of downtown district where it cost her twelve dollars for the privilege of leaving her car keys with a valet, who did nothing more than park her mini van not ten yards from the door at a curb that had meters.

She was late by at least seven minutes, due to an unforeseen car seat fiasco and two lost binkies on the way to the clinic, where she promised the receptionist, Stacy that she would only be an hour and a half and that, although child care was not in her original job description, twenty bucks said that which didn't kill you, made you stronger.

"You're a peach!" Hannah gushed as she backed out of the front door, throwing kisses and waving to Olivia, whose sticky fingers patted away at Stacy's new blouse. "There's a Barney DVD in my laptop."

"You owe me, Hannah!" Stacy said, smiling.

Buford Jones was already seated at a table in front of the restaurant, nursing a glass of ice water. He rose humbly as she rushed the table, gushing apologies. She peeled off her scarf and overcoat, fumbling awkwardly. "I'm late . . . I'm so sorry."

"Not at all," he said. They shook hands and settled in their seats. "Please, call me Buford. None of this, 'Mr. Jones' crap, okay?" His smile was warm and inviting.

She nodded. "Done, but only if you call me Hannah."

"Fair enough. Please, order what you'd like. I hear that the Cobb salad is especially good."

The waitress took their orders and disappeared. Buford commented on the benefits of beating out the lunch crowd by dining prior to noon, and then got right down to the point.

"We're interested in giving you some air time. Perhaps an hour or two on a Saturday—just to see what kind of response we'll get. You know, sort of test-drive a call-in helpline format. This would be new to our line-up, and we would need to be cautious about how we pitch this to our listeners, but that would be our problem to figure out.

All we would need you to do is be who you are. Just be Dr. Hannah."

Identical Cobb salads and two iced teas arrived. Hannah tried to remain calm and clear-headed.

"Are you offering me a *job*, Buford?"

"Yes, I am. Right now we'll continue to present you as a guest on the show and pay your professional fee, of course. You will be the 'visiting Dr. Hannah.' You can sit in on the beginning of Larry Schoestzlien's *Early Morning Rising* segment that airs from five to nine."

"*A.M.!*" Hannah gasped, stabbing the lettuce wedge with her fork.

"Hey, Doc., this is show business. It's not for the faint of heart. Larry's segment airs right before Kip and Sidney's show, followed by the mid-morning drive with Courtney Reed. She's popular with the younger set—the eighteen to twenty-four-year olds."

"Now that sounds more like my demographic."

Buford grinned like a Cheshire cat, releasing a rolling belly laugh that suggested that he should quit the smokes sometime. "Your demographic, huh? By George, I think we've created a monster here!"

Hannah blushed. Here she was, a simple housewife from Cuyahoga Falls, having lunch with the general manager of a hip radio station, who wanted *her* to guest host a talk show, dispensing advice! The thought of it all positively floored her.

"So, what do you say, Hannah? Are you game?"

"I suppose I could offer my services. And if it goes well?"

"Then we'll take a look at doing something a little more permanent. But for right now, I just want you to have fun with it. Take the hour and do what you do best. It's as simple as that."

"Okay, Buford. You got yourself an amateur host," she said, hardly believing that it was not a dream.

He grinned.

CHAPTER 14
★ ★ ★

1972

THE DRIVE TO NASHVILLE WAS the least that Keira could do after all that Hannah had done for her in the two short years that they had been friends, locker-mates, and soul sisters at heart. Graduation had been another bust, but only because Hannah had the flu and wasn't able to walk down the auditorium aisle, or toss her cap, or anything. This ritual of packing up the car and driving Hannah to her new school at the University was one that Keira was determined to deliver—even if it meant that for the next four years, they would be a seven-and-a-half-hour car ride away. Keira wanted to make Hannah's send-off as monumental as she could.

"That's her," Robert announced, jumping up from the couch when he heard the horn sound from the driveway. It was early, and he was still in his bathrobe.

Charlotte padded in her house slippers from the kitchen. "Okay, she's here! Hannah, come on down. Your friend is here!"

Keira had pulled onto the driveway and left the '65 Ford Fairlane running. She got out, leaned against the rusted door, and lit a smoke. Parents weren't her thing, and she figured that the Courtlands had the right to say their goodbyes in private.

Charlotte was already in tears when Hannah emerged with the last of her suitcases and a pillow. "I'm ready, I guess."

Robert stood up and produced a wad of bills from his housecoat. "Here's a little foldin' money for the road, just in case." Then he sniffed, and enveloped her in a giant bear hug.

"Thank you, Daddy," Hannah said, as she gave the room one long glance just to keep it locked in her photographic mind.

Charlotte stepped forward with a grocery bag full of tin foil-covered plates and warm sodas at the bottom, and handed it to Robert. "Dad will carry this out with your bags."

Hannah smiled. She was secretly glad that she had agreed to let Keira drive her. It would be better this way, with a clean goodbye. She would only be five hundred miles away.

"Okay, well, then you call when you get there, all right? Anything you've forgotten, we'll mail it to you. Be sure to eat and rest enough. You can call anytime. Just reverse the charges." Charlotte was chatting nervously, loath to let her youngest leave without the proper blessings and assurances.

"I love you guys," Hannah said, and then reached to hug them both at the same time. A few hot tears slipped from behind her new spectacles that Charlotte had said made her look scholarly. It was unavoidable. She had the most loving parents any girl could ever hope to have, and the gravity of the moment was taking her by surprise.

"I will call, I promise. Right when I get there."

"What about your friend, Keira?" Robert asked. "Will

she be staying with you?"

"She is planning on driving back tomorrow. She's a good friend."

"Well, you tell her we thank her . . . and to drive carefully." Charlotte choked on her words, now dabbing her own eyes.

"I'll walk you out," Robert said, reaching for the suitcase.

In a few minutes the car was loaded and the two girls were ready to go.

Charlotte blew a kiss from the window, and Robert stood in the driveway, tugging on his robe, watching as the car pulled onto the street.

Keira beeped the horn twice, and they sputtered off.

Hannah looked back and watched as her childhood home faded in the distance, making way for the road ahead.

CHAPTER 15
★ ★ ★

THE NURSE OPENED THE EYELET curtains, letting in the morning sun, which caused the woman to blink in protest.

"Are you going to sleep away the day?" she said, bending to give her pillow a squeeze. "Your breakfast is here." Then, helping the woman with her slippers, the large, kind nurse reached for the eyeglasses on the bureau beside the bed and placed them on the woman's face.

"Robert?" the woman said, coming out of the fog of sleep.

"Robert is on his way. Do you want some oatmeal?"

The woman's face looked pensive, and then she gave a little nod. "Sure, I can try it."

"I see that you have been working on your color books," the nurse said, tearing one of the pages from the book. "I am going to hang this one up right here on your wall, okay? How does that sound?"

The woman said nothing. She lifted the spoon and then stopped, forgetting what came next.

"I got you, Mrs. Courtland," the nurse said. "Let me help

you with that."

Charlotte nodded and smiled. "Sure."

CHAPTER 16
★ ★ ★

CLEVELAND, OHIO
2003

THE VERY NEXT WEEK BACK at the radio station, Hannah was fitted with another set of headphones—a better pair that felt snug and were more lightweight. She was introduced to a skeletal office staff and crew; polite, efficient people who had no idea who she was, but seemed to welcome her on board. It was still dark outside. The program manager, Bill Quarry, took her around the studio for a swift orientation. She would be sitting in on the first hour of Larry Schoetzlien's show, up until the weather break, for the rest of the week.

Hannah had met Courtney Reed briefly in the Green Room, where she was busily prepping for her mid-morning show with some yoga and meditation. She was a naturally slim plain-type young woman with a cherub face wearing a flowing gauze skirt. Her long brown hair was twisted like a pretzel into a thick braid that snaked down her back. The Native American woven bracelets on her tan wrists jangled when she moved, and she wore an earth crystal around her neck.

She and Hannah shook hands.

"Hi, I'm Courtney. I understand we're going to be working together. Welcome to WCLK."

"Thank you" Hannah smiled. "This is all so exciting. I've heard your show and it's very good. I hope the station's audience will be responsive to this . . . to me."

Courtney nodded, and her earrings made the sound of wind chimes. Hannah later learned that Courtney removed the noisy jewelry when she did her broadcast. This was a cardinal rule—one of many that Hannah would need to learn.

I've heard your bit with Kip and Sydney, hon. Just do what you did then and you'll be fine. Not too much psychobabble, though. Just honest-to-goodness straight talk. That's what the people want. Trust me. It works."

It worked so well that Hannah was asked to permanently replace the faltering Drew Sheltie's *Into the Night* snooze-fest, weekdays from nine p.m. until midnight. *Well Being with Dr. Hannah Courtland-Murphy* did so well in just three months time that Buford Jones approved signing her on as a resident host. She fielded everything imaginable, from dispensing divorce and break-up advice to pet loss and grief. The calls just kept coming, and it was Hannah's job to solve the pending problems in record time—a definite challenge, given the normal parameters of her home-based practice with the standard fifty-minute therapy sessions that she typically navigated in the comfort of her converted den. This was a whole new ballgame. The list of problems were unending, and could barely be understood fully in the span of two minutes or less, let alone *solved* in the speed-of-lightning thirty-second therapy session allotted for each inquiry. It was more madness than meaning, and Hannah quickly found herself offering sound bites of advice rather than insightful conversation. Consequently, her curt, quip retorts soon defined her persona as the fast-talking, no-nonsense shrink with all the answers.

The day she received her SAG card it became official. Hannah was a bona fide radio talk show host with a license to counsel listeners from a tiny stool in a booth in a high-rise near Public Square, where decisions would be made, quarrels settled, lives transformed as the tiny middle-aged mom in blue jeans gave her all, night after night, to help listeners with their problems. Hannah gave solid advice, hope, and the message of healing.

"It starts with how you think about the problem," she would tell a caller whose insomnia caused her to seek help on the airwaves. "Is what's keeping you up what's holding you back?" Hannah would ask. "Let me explain what I mean . . ."

CHAPTER 17
★ ★ ★

2003

THE NEW ROUTINE WAS GRUELING. Just when the family had finished dinner, Hannah would clean up, help Broderick with his homework, and then get Olivia ready for bed. After that, she would get herself ready to leave for the radio station. The new live-in nanny, Adelita Ortiz, had been hired to keep everything running smoothly with the added workload. She was highly recommended by one of Hannah's colleague's at the women's center. Now, with less members of the Murphy clan around, with the eldest boys living their respective college-driven lives on dual coasts, and Peter working so much overtime at the hospital, Hannah needed the full-time help.

Hannah prepped for her show earlier in the day, in between seeing patients, Olivia's nap time, and running the household errands. Peter was up and out of the house by five a.m. daily, and occasionally did not return until well after ten p.m. Needless to say, the arrangement put a strain on the marriage much earlier than then, but an unspoken tolerance for moving so completely in separate directions was continuing to be maintained. This created a larger wedge between Hannah and Peter, who soon became reduced to being roommates; seemingly, passing through the days and nights on separate trajectories. Everyone simply registered the silent compliance as status quo. This was a very unconventional family, at best.

Adelita was more than a nanny and housemaid. She was the Murphys' lifeline in keeping everything running smoothly and giving Hannah the ability to work and raise her daughter with as much consistency as possible. Plus, Olivia simply adored her. Hannah had first resisted outsourcing her domestic responsibilities any more than she absolutely had to, but the decision to bring Adelita on full-time in order to cover the many nights that Peter's work obligations kept him from coming home in time for Hannah to leave, made it necessary.

By seven-thirty p.m., Hannah was tired and spent, but somehow managed to pull herself together for another late- night show. She would shower, change, and then somehow manage to shift gears. With coffee in hand, she headed for the station with dedication few professionals could match. This was her choice. Buford Jones and the callers simply *needed* her.

She would arrive at the studio with a clearer mind by the time she drove the thirty-five miles into the city. It was an odd time to be commuting, as busy rush-hour traffic had since died down and the buildings and streets were empty. The deserted halls and corridors of the office building were left lit here and there for the cleaning crews and late-night shifters like herself. Sometimes she felt a nagging sense of guilt for sneaking out of her house after dark to do a job that was not financially necessary, but rather, something that made her feel purposeful—important. It was more than a job to Hannah. It was fast becoming a new source of identity for her. And she liked the way it made her feel to directly help others.

"Hi, Dr. Hannah. My name is Jess. I am a transgender teen." A listless voice floats across the airwaves. "I'm keeping my voice down. I don't want my stepdad to know I'm calling you."

"Are you in a safe place, Jess?" Hannah says, punching up the volume a bit on her headset.

"Yeah, I'm in my room. The TV is on. He can't hear." The caller swallows hard and goes on. "The thing is . . . he hates the sight of me. He always has. He calls me names like 'tranny boy,' and he's—"

"He's *what*, Jess?"

Dead air. Then the sound is muffled. Finally, the caller breathes, "Once. He threw a pan of bacon grease at me for wearing eyeliner."

"Are you hurt? I mean, right now. Are you in any danger, Jess?" Hannah bridges the question skillfully.

"No. He's only done that once. He hates me, though. He hits my mom when she defends me."

"Listen to me, Jess. Can you leave the house? Is there someone you can confide in? Are you in middle school or high school?" Hannah asks.

"I'm a junior."

"Do you have a teacher or counselor that you feel that you could talk to? Who might that be?"

"I have an English teacher, Ms. Paddock. She's nice. I wrote about this in an essay that I handed in, and she asked me about it. I told her that I made it up."

"Why did you do that? Lie, I mean?" Hannah asks.

"This thing that happened to you—when your stepdad threw the bacon grease. Did you tell anyone else other than Ms. Paddock?"

"No. Not until now. I didn't want her to report it."

"Do you feel unsafe?"

"Sometimes. Yeah, usually. I guess I just wanted to see if anyone cared. I don't know how to make him stop hating me."

Hannah bristled. The teacher should have, by law, reported the incident of suspected abuse. It was a matter that would be better solved off the airwaves. She scrawls on a notepad and lifts it up to signal her producer: GET HIS NUMBER.

"Jess, I am going to ask you to wait while I go to break, okay?" Hannah says, and quickly cuts to a commercial. There would be no spectacle of a minor who was in need of intervention. Hannah would call Child Protection Services herself and report the incident and the errant teacher. It was not always easy or glamorous work. Often, it broke her heart.

"Let's check in with a caller who is looking to find love again at fifty, caller are you there?"

"Yes, I am here, Dr. Hannah. My name is Debbie. I'm newly divorced and terrified of getting out there again. Any advice for the forlorn at fifty?"

"Well, the first thing I would ask is why should anyone choose you over a younger prospect? What do *you* bring to the table in a relationship? I'm sure if you think hard enough, you will be able to come up with the upside." Hannah had a method for everything. "Let's role-play your response to that question. I'm a potential suitor, and you're going to convince me that you are more than an average catch. *Let's go—!*"

And so it went.

Hannah would return home in time to grab a few hours of sleep before Broderick, her third born, would get up for school and Olivia would be calling for her cartoons and morning juice cup. Hannah was there when Broderick came home in the afternoon, or after his part-time job at the mall, to hear about his day over dinner, which was more than she could say for Peter. He always seemed to be on call, running off to the hospital, constantly tending to one crisis or another. This fact, most probably, served as the basis for her mounting feelings of guilt. She wondered apprehensively if, with Peter never around, she should try to make up for his absence in some way.

She did manage to continue to see some choice clients during the afternoons, but made it a point to clear her calendar on weekends to dedicate to her family. Without Peter's support, though, she held completely the sole task of arranging their family outings, keeping the care packages going out to Ty and Marc to their dual-coast campuses, and planning fun excursions for Broderick and Olivia. When she did plan a family vacation at summer breaks, Peter was unable to join them, spending time, instead, immersed in his job at the hospital and climbing the corporate ranks. This made Hannah feel more like a widow than a wife.

One unfortunate time, Peter left them all midway through a four-day trip to Disneyland to attend a nearby symposium, saying, "I'm so sorry, but my hands are tied. Goddamn hospital politics. I won't be able to fly back with you and the kids."

No one was more disappointed than Hannah, who was standing by watching with a horrified dread as her marriage and family slowly shrank, bit by bit. She began to take a hard look at herself. *It's not me, personally, or the work,* she reasoned to herself. *Peter has never been prouder of my accomplishments.* It was something far less definitive, yet she could not figure it out. Instead, it seemed easier to imagine that her unconventional career was the thing that was pushing him away.

For the sake of her sanity and the stability of her family, Hannah continuously chose to make up the deficits where she could when Peter buried himself deep within his work, preening his career, cultivating connections and working double shifts with aspirations for higher management. *He deserved it, didn't he?* She encouraged his success with willful support, even though it meant having less and less of Peter for all of them. *It would just be until he made chief resident,* she would tell herself.

Even back when the boys were young, she was the one who oiled Ty's mitt for practice, re-wired a Game Boy on the fritz, or assembled a tricycle at daybreak on a snowy Christmas morning, when Peter was grounded in Denver and Santa Claus just could not wait. She recalled sitting beneath the Christmas tree that she had to purchase and tie to the roof of the Volvo with three excited children in tow, wondering to herself it all was worth sacrificing just to keep up with the Joneses. It seemed that it had always been a struggle, back as far as when Peter first started his residency. What happened to the young lovers who once could not spend one night apart?

She had remembered long afternoons spent when they were first married and had moved back to Ohio, just she and Peter, traversing the Cuyahoga River in a fiberglass canoe on a long, lazy six-mile float. Or, hiking the trails of Cascade Valley and stopping to picnic at Canal Park. She remembered his loving glances and his eagerness to please her at every turn. *Was it ever real?* she'd wondered, or just something she had imagined? No, she was certain that they had found in each other what her mother and father had once had—and still did, even though Charlotte had been wrestling with the debilitating effects of dementia for the past sixteen years. Still, Robert cared for her as if she were a child, tending to her every need and filling in the gaps of her fading and failing mind that seemed to grow worse with the passing years. There were no limits to love as far as Robert Courtland was concerned, and he not only preached this fact, he lived it. Would she and Peter ever know that kind of devotion? In sickness and in health, for better or for worse? Hannah realized that she could not answer her own question, and the reality of that terrified her.

She told herself that she would talk with Peter about it as soon as he returned. After all, she could dispense advice to strangers, why not heed what she knew was the best course of action? When the time was right, she would do it. Unfortunately, the right time never seemed to come.

It did not keep Hannah from crying when no one was looking. Moments of total breakdown and dread enveloped her as she fought to keep the momentum of the life they had created going. Sometimes it would hit her in the studio, just after a show, when the phone lights went out and the microphone cooled. Other times while she was driving home in the early hours, pulling into the driveway, or crawling into an empty bed; rising with the pre-dawn haze only to find that Peter never even made it home to bed. Again.

There was little trace of him, except for the deposit of dirty laundry left routinely in a heap on the bedroom floor or randomly timed text messages or voice mails that begged off dinner for one reason or another. They made love so sporadically that Hannah did not even bother to refill her prescription contraceptives. Her periods were becoming more and more erratic in concert with her age and in relation to the stressful demands she had placed on her changing body.

Whenever they did make love, Peter used a condom. The ritual took less than sixty seconds from snap to finish. Still, she could not help but feel so utterly slighted by the whole ordeal, as if she were not even there at all. He would simply roll on top of her, bury his face in the pillow, and pump away mechanically until, at last, he released with a contented sigh. After which, he would promptly head to the sink to wash himself.

Once, when they were having sex, she did not make a single move throughout, but he never even noticed—nor did he note the fact that she had been crying the entire time. That was the definitive moment she had known that it was over. The insightful Dr. Hannah knew what her gut had been dreading. The realization that she was in a loveless marriage.

Unfortunately, it would be twelve more years before she actually ended it.

CHAPTER 18
★ ★ ★

HANNAH PULLED ONTO THE WINDING driveway of the two-story Colonial-style home that looked more like it belonged to a broker or lawyer than a private healthcare provider. It was a group home nestled in the pristine and tranquil woods near the Cuyahoga Valley National Forest, and it had the most assuring of names—Serenity Lane. It had taken Hannah weeks to find the ideal location in which to entrust her treasured mother, Charlotte, in the care of strangers. It had been time. Robert had long been increasingly unable to care for Charlotte's needs any longer as the throes of the disease had progressed, rendering her incapable of being left alone for any length of time. It had already been six years, and Hannah never missed a daily visit or phone call, even knowing that Charlotte was in the best of care. It was Hannah's father, Robert, however, who concerned her most these days.

The decision to place Charlotte in a residential facility came after a long and loving road of at-home care and daily devotion supplied by Charlotte's loving husband of forty-two years. It was he who first noticed the changes in his beloved wife back in 1987, which were subtle at the

start, suggesting that at only age sixty, the hand of time had
begun to press upon her beautiful and sharp mind with the
hazy fog of occasional forgetfulness and the loss of a word,
or the vexatious misplacement of her car keys. Robert and
the family had come to regard the occurrences as nothing
more than the natural progress of aging, although it did
seem to worsen with each passing year.

Once, Hannah recalled mixing up a batch of dough for
Christmas crullers, which were delicious oil-fried con-
fections that when cooled, literally melted on the tongue.
It was one of Charlotte's famed traditions. The ritual was
one that they had enjoyed since Hannah could remember;
before she was even old enough to manage the ancient
rolling pin used to flatten the dough. It was an heirloom
that had once proudly belonged to Charlotte's mother,
brought to Ohio straight from the Old Country, along with
the revered recipe. It was Hannah's hope that three-year-
old Olivia would have the opportunity to one day make
the crullers with her—three generations of Courtland
women tangling in a mess of powdered sugar and laughter,
cracking eggs and pouring out the love and Myers's Rum
(Grandma Charlotte's secret ingredient) into the batches
of loving delight. Sadly, she would never have the opportunity, as Charlotte, who had already been placed at Serenity
Lane three years before Olivia was born, simply was incapable of it. It was the Christmas of 1992 when Hannah
had first noticed "mistakes" Charlotte was making, namely
mixing up the flour with the salt and the pained look on
her face when she had stopped abruptly and simply stared
off into space. It was the last time that they would make
the crullers together as each passing year robbed them of
so much more than a cherished cookie recipe.

Over the years that followed, Charlotte had grown further
confused and disoriented on a regular basis. What started as

a gradual lapse of cognition when playing a board game, or mahjong with her lady friends, led to minor scrapes on the car and missing pocketbooks. Charlotte eventually began to lose track of dates and days of the week. Occasionally, she would wander off in the supermarket or at night, once even ending up in her nightclothes standing in the middle of the backyard. Robert had to coax her back into bed after she struck him in the face for touching her. He cried for days when she asked who the man in their wedding picture was in the winter of 1997. The call that came to Hannah in the night was one she would never forget. Her father's haunting sobs, once again, breaking her heart in two. "I'm coming there now, Dad."

The next several weeks were spent seeing doctors and performing standard blood tests and examinations. Charlotte underwent countless cognitive assessments—memory tests, problem-solving puzzles, counting and language drills. These were followed by physical tests including brain scans, computer topography, and magnetic resonance imaging to rule out other possible causes or symptoms. Family members were asked to answer a battery of questions that even for Hannah, seemed excessive, all revolving around Charlotte's health and changes in her behavior. Many of the inquiries, Hannah regrettably could not answer. She had been so busy with juggling her own life, graduate school, her job at the counseling center, and her husband's often distant, brooding behavior that she was not able to attest to her mother's mental acuity. Conversations with her siblings revealed even less, as Muriel, the eldest, was off teaching at a professorship out of the country and her brother, Robert Jr., was somewhere in Utah, navigating his own mid-life crisis in an RV with his two German Shepherds and girl-friend of-the-moment in tow.

Hannah was relieved to learn that Robert had kept numerous journals all throughout his and Charlotte's married life, which included his deep and distressful angst at watching his beloved slip away in the passing years, bit by bit, chronicled in explicit detail.

"Dad, you are so amazing. These stories are so wonderful." Hannah pored over the box of bounded volumes, journals and spiral notebooks. "You kept it all. Everything, from the beginning." She smiled, wiping a tear from her cheek.

The love story of Charlotte and Robert Courtland was nothing short of remarkable. Hannah had always known it. But now, the past several years had revealed a story of a different kind; one that recorded the changes in her mother in vivid detail. Everything was there—the decline, starting in June of 1992, when she was forgetting to pay the monthly bills, putting things in unusual places, and finally, the minor car wreck at the mall. Then, in 1995, when they took away her car keys, she began to grow confused and suspicious, depressed and fearful. She lashed out at Robert, thinking at times that he was a stranger, or calling the police to report a break-in when once the chicken thawing on the kitchen counter, according to her, went missing.

Charlotte could not be easily comforted. Even the decision to hire in-home help from a respite care center providing Robert with assistance tending to his wife's many needs bathing, toileting, dressing, and remaining mobile became increasingly more difficult for Robert to bear. Regular visits to an adult care facility seemed to be the one thing that brightened Charlotte's mood. They had arranged to take her to the center twice a week to experience planned activities with other patients who were in various stages of Alzheimer's disease, which was what the test results had determined was Charlotte's fate. Remarkably, the planned activities, particularly the music and art programs, reached Charlotte in a way that nothing and nobody else could. It caused her to smile and close her eyes, summoning up some distant memory, perhaps of her and her sweetheart, somewhere frozen back in time. Robert got her a small recorder and loaded cassette tapes with old songs and stories recorded in his own voice taken from his journals of their meeting, courtship, and incredible life and love for one another.

Charlotte would sit and listen for hours on end. It was medicine for her soul.

Hannah was an advocate first for holistic and natural remedies, where they could be substituted for drugs and medication. It had become evident, though, that Charlotte would benefit from the advances available to soothe her anxieties and give her a sense of comfort and security. This, along with a full-time care facility that shared in her and Robert's vision for the highest of care, was in order. Serenity Lane provided just that. A state-of-the-art facility with a focus on nutrition, physical activity, social engagement, and mentally stimulating pursuits. This was the place. Hannah knew it the first moment she pulled up to the sprawling landscape with its inviting pink and purple lilacs lining the garden paths with their delicate, heart-shaped leaves and pastel blooms. It was more than just a skilled care facility—it was a caring home. And her mother deserved no less.

Hannah stood in the doorway and watched as the frail, bent woman who was once a vibrant and elegant dancer sat still in the rocking chair, facing the window and watching the western sunset. A tiny music box glistened atop an antique bureau, and a bright granny square afghan was folded neatly at the foot of the bed. Evenings were the hardest and would bring agitation, disorientation, and confusion. Robert had stepped out for his dinner, but would be back in time to assist Charlotte with hers. Then, he would sit by her bedside as she dozed, at the ready to respond if she called out or needed him. Hannah would take the pre-dinner shift when she could and sit with her mother, never knowing if the time would be spent soothing her fears, or conversing with her like a friendly stranger, chatting about the weather or the bluebells that were sure to bloom sweet and steady with the spring rains.

It was in those moments when Hannah cared not about keeping callers to less than three minutes, the empty nest syndrome that had left two holes where once Ty and Marc had nestled, Olivia's toddler tantrums, or the stabs of insecurity that threatened to pierce the heart of her failing marriage. In those moments there with Charlotte, sharing tea and placid glances, she was at peace, knowing that it was she who was being cared for by the most important person in the world, not the other way around.

CHAPTER 19
★ ★ ★

2004

"*HELLO. THIS IS* THE DR. Hannah Show—*and you're on the air . . .*"

It was not long before a cult following ushered Hannah's show top of ratings, eliciting requests from listeners who wanted more of the good doctor's potion. The emails and message board comments declared what Buford Jones had predicted—*"More Dr. Hannah!"*

So, Jones awarded Hannah her own time slot, from four a.m. to seven a.m. each weekday. Here, callers sought counsel, truth, and thirty seconds or more of fame, as their private lives were made public across the airwaves, asking the good doctor to shed some light on their darkest dilemmas.

"I work third shift at the factory, and listen to Dr. Hannah on my breaks. She is an expert on problems I can relate to."

"She starts my day with a stiff shot of the truth. She pulls no punches!"

"Dr. Hannah, thank you for your sensible advice. You were spot-on about how my husband's toxic behavior is holding us all hostage. The cycle changes today!"

The callers would gush their sentiments resoundingly. *"I love your show! I listen all the time and could use your advice on a little problem I'm having with my live-in lover/wife/landlord/ pet snake—."* You name it. They pitched every problem and quandary known to man, woman, child, or beast. The show's producers had heard it all.

And listen they did, screening thousands of calls, letters, and emails from an anxious and adoring public; listeners looking for old-fashioned sound advice. Some, in search of a kind word, or tongue-lashing, if need be—all for the cost of a single phone call. It was sound therapy on a dime.

It was a long way from the days of crisis center counseling and offering cookie-recipe therapy in her kitchen, or scribbling on a legal pad in her den while a bereaved divorcee lamented the trials of facing life as a single middle-aged mom. The problems were still served up, only now at lightning-fast speed—and in a world that took mental health advice quickly dispensed over the airwaves on their car radios, stereo consoles, and portable devices. The world was changing indeed, but human beings were still basically the same: fearful, damaged, hopeful. And turn to her they did in numbers. Numbers that amounted to profits.

In spring of 2004, Jones signed Hannah on to a two-year contract, putting her three-hour show further into the limelight, offering her Courtney Reed's chair in the highly coveted mid-day timeslot, causing the listenership numbers to skyrocket. By measure of the sudden increase in sheer volume of callers flooding the phone lines of WCLK, everyone delighted in the obvious triumph of Hannah's unprecedented bold, take-no-prisoners personality, along with her spot-on sage advice.

And so it was—a talk radio star was born.

CHAPTER 20
★ ★ ★

PITTSBURGH, PENNSYLVANIA
2005

IT WAS THE FOURTH TUESDAY of the month and only the second time that Peter had been brave enough to walk into the club after chickening out so many times before. He had noticed him working behind the bar the previous time he had slinked into the hazy half-light. They had crossed paths once when he was on the way to use the john. That night, Peter had stopped and leaned against the bar to linger, feeling something very distinctively different as he watched the blond-haired, attractive man wiping out the shot glasses and chatting with the patrons, noticing his name tag that read Anthony. Peter felt it again, only stronger, when he followed him on his way out of the bar into the parking lot right as the club was closing. He did not know what made him do it, but he slipped his business card nonchalantly under the windshield wiper of Anthony's yellow jeep the next night on his way to the airport to catch a flight back home to his normal life.

Three weeks later, when Anthony called on Peter's private line at the office, his stomach did flips and he had to excuse himself as having to check on a patient in order to compose himself. The gorgeous boy stammered nervously himself when, a day later, he left a coy message on Peter's voice mail, asking him to meet him the following Tuesday at an upscale dinner club on the south side of Pittsburgh, renowned in gay circles for its discretionary dark windows. The restaurant was attached to a four-star hotel with satin sheets, an oversize Jacuzzi, and complimentary champagne in-room dinner service for its discreet patrons.

Peter vomited into the commode just minutes after ejaculating into Anthony's mouth, only to find himself in the weeks that followed, unable to get the young man and the thought of having sex with him, out of his mind.

Peter had returned for months to follow, finding every excuse possible to go to Pennsylvania, as well as reasons not to go. Once at home surrounded by his loving, picture-perfect family and thriving practice, he did not have to look very far.

Still, he maintained a duo life. Under the guise of work or research, he returned to Pittsburgh and to Anthony time and again. Soon, one year turned into two, and two eventually into five.

CHAPTER 21
★ ★ ★

NEW YORK CITY, NY
2015

HANNAH STARED AT THE CURSOR blinking on the screen. Then, she surveyed her desk. Every award, every accolade seemed in the half-light to mock her. She closed her eyes and measured her breathing. In the decade that had followed, "Dr. Hannah" had became a household name, and not least of all—party to Americans' insatiable quick-fix obsession for mental guidance *to go*, streaming on their car radios, laptops, and smartphones. Unique to the high- profile pop-psychologist was a compelling persona and a quick wit that made her unique, engaging style addictive to listen to. Her banter with the callers was high-spirited, informative, funny, and direct. In the business of radio, each call had to be executed quickly, fitting neatly within the allotted package of precise time restraints. As a result, Dr. Hannah had to deliver her expert gems of advice in a window of no less than three and a half minutes per call—sometimes less; a constraint that drove her to compromise her bedside manner in order to get rather directly to the point on any given call. And damn the niceties of the "other" talk host geniuses who had time to spare!

Hannah had to identify each problem right out of the gate, often appearing to badger the poor caller with questions and requests for background information in order to set up a viable solution, and sometimes cutting them off mid-sentence to deliver her verdict.

"Dump him! Fess up! Get real!"

"Apologize, or be prepared to revisit this issue."

"Walk away . . . "

Hannah quickly began earning the reputation of being a no-nonsense, hard-nosed shrink shorter on the sugar of her previous methods and long on dispensing straightforward, brutally honest advice. The kind of advice that helped listeners to turn their lives around for the better—and continue to grow the ratings in the process.

She had become a seasoned businesswoman. A commodity.

Dr. Hannah was a hit with the sponsors, who clamored to purchase airtime that would have her endorse their products. She touted everything from fitness bikes to age cream. Her word was credible, her advice strong and solid.

She was a symbol of conscience and integrity, vying for truth over folly, and not afraid to chastise her own audience for being too self-serving and narcissistic, saying, *"I won't tell you what you want to hear."* She would besiege a whiny caller weighing the ramifications of choosing between his twenty-seven-year-old secretary and his thirty-year marriage. *You made a commitment, which alone leaves you without a choice, does it not? What's the problem then, Roy? Dump the floozy who's wrecking your castle! Think with your head—it's the reason you have one."*

Click.

"Next caller, please. Hello. This is Dr. Hannah . . . Arlene, why

don't you tell me why *you have a problem with the fact that your daughter is a lesbian?"*

Three hours a day Hannah dispensed advice concerning life's colorful spectrum from the lovelorn to the lost; the addicted to the conflicted. Dr. Hannah's shingle swung, covering the gamut of human behavior and dysfunction; solving family squabbles, building bridges, tearing down walls, and always putting forth the underlying belief that the power to heal is within everyone. And that righteousness and goodness reside in every man and woman alive.

Dr. Hannah extolled the power of inner strength, as well as heavenly faith, *"I'm just here to help remind you of it. God gave you the tools you need. Take yourself out of the equation."*

This answer satisfied the masses, offering "God" to mean the faith-source or deity most identified by each individual listener.

While Dr. Hannah was known to expound controversially, *"The holy bible is the only rule book in life you'll ever need,"* she did manage to pen several best-sellers of her own in the years that followed. These were a series of four self-help paperbacks extolling the benefits of living life high on virtue and personal honor; avoiding the derailing pitfalls of greed and selfishness. These were reminiscent of her maternal approach to preaching morality, and as expected, packed a punch: *Moral Fiber, More Moral Fiber, Moral Fiber for Teens,* and *Band-Aids for the Broken Soul.*

Eventually, Dr. Hannah became a frequent keynote speaker at numerous symposiums and charity events that raised money to fund safe houses and women's advocacy programs nationally. She was a champion for mental health and child welfare outreach programs; supported countless organizations that sought to lend her name to needy and laudable causes. Dr. Hannah was a bleeding heart, and no amount of fame or notoriety would change that. She was a wife and a mother first and foremost, reminding herself unceasingly that the greatest title and honor in her life was that of being a mom—"Dr. Mom" not only to her family but to her adoring listeners, a moniker that was aptly exploited by the broadcasting conglomerate's marketing team.

Now, at age sixty, however, right then and there, it hit her. She would be facing the prospect of life as a divorced woman herself—the one and only blemish on an otherwise perfect career and virtually flawless life. Over the past several decades, she had raised four perfect children, three of whom were grown and successful in their own right; she had won numerous awards, written books, had a thriving practice, and had gained notoriety anchoring what had become the number-one-rated syndicated radio talk show in the country. But the biggest honor in her life was being grandmother to two beautiful granddaughters. And now, here she was about to send them—the light of her very life— their morning joke. Why, then, did she feel like she was dying inside?

CHAPTER 22

★ ★ ★

2005

IT WAS NOT ALWAYS PURPLE furs and fancy handbags for Marney Valentine. An adult since the tender age of seventeen, she had been around the block and back by the time she turned twenty-one, when she left her east Brooklyn neighborhood at age ten, to live with an aunt in Greenwich Village who had a bad string of battering boyfriends and a nasty drug addiction. There was never a mother to speak of. Her father, Chad Warinski, was a former musician-turned concert promoter for Manhattan Records, who traveled two hundred days out of the year. Marney was his only daughter, from wife number three. She had six siblings, total—one natural-born brother, and five stepbrothers who lived with various relatives through-out the country. Chad had pawned Marney off on his sister, Rebecca, until she started getting restless around age thirteen.

It was then that Chad would take Marney along with him on band tours, exposing her to the hard-core, uncensored realities of the music business and of life on the concert circuit. The wanton lifestyle was an unfortunate upshot of his profession.

Marney grew up on a tour bus, getting hit on by everything from roadies to rockers. And, not unremarkably, she could sing. She had gargantuan-size talent, and Chad hoped to cash in on it big time, by exploiting her any way that he could.

He forced her on record agents, distribution managers, songwriters, producers, and club owners—anyone who would listen—dressing her provocatively in spandex leotards and too-tight designer jeans. He loaded on the mascara and blush and tried to pass her off as being eighteen when she was barely fifteen.

She hated every minute of it. Mostly, the unwanted stares and advances of every long-haired, coked-out, band freak who promised they could make her a star.

Most of all, she hated Chad for selling her out.

She lost her virginity to a guy named Zip, who wore eye makeup and a nose stud, on a couch in a dressing room, somewhere in Pittsburgh. *It doesn't get more pathetic than that,* Marney often thought, whenever she recalled those dark, dark days. Even living with her strung-out Aunt Rebecca in a cockroach-infested studio flat was better than watching life and truck stops go by in the rearview mirror of a production bus. She was not cut out for the lifestyle that ultimately drove her own worthless father to despair and destruction.

So at sixteen, she took one hundred twenty dollars—all she had in crumpled bills—and caught a Greyhound straight back to Brooklyn and to Aunt Rebecca's, where another hellish slice of life awaited.

Chad Warinski lived a jaded, pathetic existence, immersed in a cesspool of drugs, fast living, and carnal pleasures untold, pining from the sidelines for his day in the spotlight. Ironically, he managed to take his own life before the booze and the barbiturates did him in, hanging himself from a scaffold of can lights before a Stones concert in Madison Square Garden. He was, to his detriment, remembered only for the contribution his suicide had lent to the holdup of the show, delaying the curtain for fifty minutes while authorities removed the body. It was a stunt, which in turn, coined a new buzz phrase in the entertainment sector. From that point on, the term "pulling a Warinski" applied whenever technical or other complications held off the timely start of any show.

Marney miraculously managed to finish high school, pushing herself to work two jobs at one time, while taking night classes at a local community college in order to save enough money to get out on her own. She found a less cockroach-infested garden apartment, which she shared with an exchange student, a bartender, and a female impersonator, who soon disappeared, unsurprisingly, stiffing them all on the rent. The only consolation being that he/she left behind a fantastic trunk of fabulous clothes that Marney helped herself to. The apartment was located on Manhattan's east side and had a walled-in view of a concrete courtyard. It was sub-adequate by anyone's standards, but Marney loved it.

At age twenty, she committed what she deemed to be a cardinal sin. Against her own better judgment, she met and married a musician. He was a rock 'n' roll flunky who called himself Sir Kenny. Her commitment to the marriage ended before it even began, as suspicion of Kenny's penchant for infidelity was confirmed when Marney found him bedding her maid of honor five days before the wedding; a practice that he entertained equally enthusiastically during their ill-advised marriage.

Kenny's band, Cobra City, had just signed a record deal with Atlantic, and who was she to walk out on a sixty-five- percent cut of her beloved's profits? The way she saw things, she'd earned it.

So, Marney stayed in just long enough for Cobra to climb just short of the chart's top forty with a rad metal ballad, "Virgin Bride." It put the band on the map, and launched Cobra on an eighteen-month international tour. The band sold half a million records, enough for Marney to make Kenny give until it hurt.

She sent a fax to his dressing room in Amsterdam with photos taken herself, of his tryst with the blushing brides-maid and several other jail-bait poster groupies for good measure, laid spread-eagle beneath his royal bastardness. Who was, incidentally, still wearing his signature black sleeveless leather vest while he was doing the deed, expos-ing, among other things, the indisputable ink tattoo of a coiling reptile trademark spelling out the word, C-O-B-R-A around his meaty bicep. Lawyers were retained, and a swift and quiet settlement was granted.

She gave up the slug, but kept her married surname, *Val-entine*, which had a kind of an edgy efficacy.

With proceeds from her divorce, Marney quit her self-declared job as a "part-time songwriter" and banked her settlement. It was time, she concluded, to fashion a *real* career of her own. Long on determination, she obtained a business degree from Columbia in upstate New York, and then decided to put it to good use. Following a childhood passion of sorts, she had a flair for theatrics, a keen and unorthodox sense of style, and when somebody wanted to throw a soirée of event proportions, they called on Marney to deliver. So, naturally, she started her own event-planning company.

Small and strictly by word of mouth, Marney's business began to grow exponentially in the late '90s. She assisted friends and colleagues with the logistics and countless cre-ative details of planning their weddings, birthdays, club openings, book signings, corporate receptions, and even pet birthday parties—gratis at first, just to get her feet wet. You name it, Marney lent her touch to producing high-style, to-die-for invites that not only got people talking, but also got her noticed. Soon her phone was ringing off the hook with requests for Marney's Marvelous Events! LLC.

She was a one-woman show with minimal overhead, and eventually a prestigious upper west side address in a trendy Manhattan studio just off West 59th Street that she shared with a dubious accident lawyer. It was the size of a dorm room, with less potential. It barely housed two desks that were actually card tables, a fax machine, a copier, and an anemic client Rolodex that would eventually grow to be a remarkable quarter of a million dollars a year sales commodity.

Marney did it all from the confines of the small office. She orchestrated caterers and wait staff; hired equipment vendors, florists, scenic designers, and procured tent and event companies to transform ballrooms into backyards, and backyards into ballrooms, or outback posts, 1920s style speakeasies, or any other desired fabrication of her client's imagination and budget. Marney threw a great party. It was as simple as that.

In just three short years, Marney sold off the business and parlayed her prestigious connections and predilection as a dealmaker to take an opportunity that landed her a dream job. She accepted an offer with a renowned public relations firm, where she built a reputation for promoting some of New York's most notable talent. The firm's portfolio boasted over fifty prominent clients. Marney coordinated interviews and personal appearances, radio and TV spots, print ads, as well as film engagements over the following years for a bevy of high-profile politicians and celebrities.

In the spring of 2002 she quit the firm to break out on her own, forming a private public relations agency called

Marney Valentine, Inc. She had exclusive representation
of a sports anchor named Sammy Keyes from Milwau-
kee who broadcasted weekdays at a local TV network; five
voice-over actors, two male underwear models, a commercial actress, a fourteen-year-old pro tennis prima donna, a
nationally acclaimed stand-up comic who had just landed a
gratuitous appearance on *Late Night* with Conan O'Brien
as a favor from an undisclosed connection that she took
credit for. Marney never shared her trade secrets and was
always looking to land top talent, as good clients seemed to
come and go with the whims of media contracts and the
public's fickle temperaments.

And now, Marney was about to make Dr. Hannah Courtland-Murphy her crowning jewel. She had learned of
Hannah's quickly rising popularity and notable impact on
the station's and network's skyrocketing ratings throughout the country. Hannah's steady increase in cumulative
audience reach was impressive indeed. Steady spikes in listenership and extended high mid-day rankings were just
what advertisers were looking for. Hannah had staying
power. Marney was certain of it. And she was dead certain
that she could definitely use a good, controversial radio
personality with high-level appeal to round out her client
roster. Dr. Hannah also was, in her opinion, badly in need
of an image makeover, which was Marney's specialty. She
knew that she could repackage and sell the entire brand of
Dr. Hannah's unique appeal, undeniable talent, and chutzpah. The radio shrink was definitely in need of a little help,
and Marney was at the ready to provide.

A quick inquiry on the subject revealed that Hannah
did not have exclusive representation, and that, not surprisingly, a West Coast agency was sniffing around as well
for the opportunity to sign her. She would have to act fast
if she was going to "court" Hannah. And so she set out to

do just that.

CHAPTER 23
★ ★ ★

FALL 2005

HANNAH ARRIVED HOME ONE AFTERNOON following her broadcast. She had stopped to take care of some errands and was running later than usual. The house was quiet, and no one seemed to be home. She kicked her shoes off in the front hall and scooped up the stack of mail on the credenza. It had been a long day already, and she was exhausted. A hot bath and a cup of Adelita's vegetable soup, which she could smell wafting from the kitchen, sounded heavenly. She padded to the kitchen in her stocking feet and noticed through the back door that she was not entirely alone.

Adelita was sitting on the patio having a smoke. She saw Hannah and quickly snuffed the cigarette into a flowerpot.

"Mrs. Hannah, I have your dinner now," she said with comforting eyes.

"Where is everyone?" Hannah asked.

"Dr. Peter . . . he took Broderick and little Olivia to the skate park today. He say, he tol' ju yesterday, I think."

"I'm sure he did not." Hannah puzzled. Had she been working so much lately that she could not remember even the simplest things, like the whereabouts of her family? It was getting dark. "Did Peter say when they would be back?"

Adelita looked pained. Mrs. Murphy was getting angry and she really hated being caught in the middle of one of Dr. and Mrs. Murphy's disputes.

The front door swung open, and in traipsed her tired and spirited crew. Olivia was fast asleep in Peter's arms from exhaustion.

"Hey, Mom!" Broderick said holding up his skateboard. "You missed out. It was so rad—I finally did an Ollie on the park ramp. Shredded it! Next time, I'm gonna add a kick flip. You should have seen how much air I got! It was *sick*."

Hannah turned up the lights and shot Peter a telling glare. "Can I see you a minute, Peter? Broderick, go finish your homework, please. And no computer games until you're done. I do want to see that trick, though, next time," she said, calling after his now-retreating back.

Peter handed Olivia off into Adelita's ready arms. "I take her upstairs to bed," she said sheepishly.

"Thank you, Adelita." Hannah was appreciative. "I'll be right up." The woman's house cleaning was questionable, but she was a dream with Olivia.

Hannah followed Peter further into the kitchen and addressed her husband sternly.

"A skate park? I hope that you made Broderick wear his helmet. Why on earth didn't you call to tell me what you were all doing? Did they even eat dinner yet? There's school tomorrow, and—"

"And what, Hannah? We grabbed some tacos from the food truck at the park. And yes, he wore his helmet, and his elbow pads, and his kneepads. It was not a big deal. I'm sorry I didn't call. Obviously, I had my hands full. *God-*

dammit! I've been out of town every weekend for three months straight. I just wanted to spend some time with them. Since when is that a crime?"

"I didn't say that it was," Hannah's said.

He racked through his hair, which was cut short near his temples; now a brassy auburn, mixed with streaks of gray where the boyish highlights once were. Hannah wondered how a man working so many hours a month had a tan like a seasoned golfer. She was jealous of the freedom he had taking the afternoon off from work like this and running off to the park with the kids. More importantly—without *her*. Her life lately did not afford such luxuries.

"Oh, save it, Hannah. Save it for your callers."

He said the word as if it was a bad thing. *Callers.* As if they were an addiction or a disease. Either way, the connotation was unfair and harsh. He knew it.

She took the hit directly where it was aimed, at her heart.

Then came a tougher blow. "Those kids are missing a hell of a lot more than a day at the park from you."

She balked at his growing anger. "What's that supposed to mean?"

"You're gone half the time—twelve to fifteen hours a day sometimes, for remote broadcasts, promotions, and station meetings—doing whatever they tell you to do."

"How dare you?" She glared.

He grabbed a beer from the fridge, flung the twist top into the sink, and then headed outside onto the deck and fresher air.

She followed, hot on his heels. "You're gone half the time at the hospital and the other half traveling to God knows where for God knows what. You missed both Ty's and Marc's graduations, which nearly broke their hearts. They would never tell you, but it did. You had made promises multiple times to go to their schools and see them."

Both boys were ensconced in their graduate studies, Ty at Duke University and Marc out West at USC. "Time is marching on, and you can never get that back. Peter, if anyone should be realistic about who's doing or not doing what, it ought to be you."

He shifted against the wood railing, turning away from her. Hannah felt her body tense from head to toe. Months of pent-up anger welled inside her. She would have to be careful, watch her words, or she was liable to say something they both would regret.

"I just know that they miss you a lot. That's all." Her voice softened. "What about us, Peter? Where are we? What's happening here?"

The questions remained unanswered in the darkness of the quiet night. Olivia had awakened and was calling for Hannah, despite Adelita's efforts to comfort her.

Hannah's pleading gaze did little to penetrate Peter's stone expression.

"How about we talk on Sunday?" he said. "My parents are coming in and can visit with Olivia for a couple of hours. Maybe take her to the zoo."

She touched his arm tentatively. "Why not sooner? Tomorrow? We can work through this, right?" Hannah's voice pleaded.

Peter wagged his head. "Can't. I'm off to Philly in the morning. I have a meeting."

"I see," Hannah's voice trailed. The feeling in the pit of her stomach told her more than he ever would. It was the fifth such trip to Philadelphia in several months.

"We'll talk when I get back. Okay?"

His Blackberry sounded from his belt loop, and he grabbed it routinely, assessing the message on the monochrome screen. "It's the hospital. Probably the triple bypass," he guessed, quickly using the scroll wheel to cue up the number. He would call to notify them that he would be on his way.

Hannah turned and started upstairs, not noticing that the number he selected was not even in Ohio.

"*I need you, Peter . . .*" a voice pleaded on the other end of the line.

"I'll be there tomorrow night," Peter whispered. "I promise you—it'll be okay."

CHAPTER 24
★ ★ ★

PITTSBURGH. PENNSYLVANIA

PETER HAD TAKEN UP A secret residence in Pittsburgh in 2005—and thus began his duo life—there with Anthony and his sometime-roommate Paul, who fancied wearing women's clothes and prancing around the apartment in large brassieres and pantyhose. By day, Paul was an unassuming two-hundred-fifty-pound commodities broker with a bad haircut and a lisp. He was, remarkably, a decent cook. Oh, would Peter's hard-nosed moral-mannered wife flip out if she could see them all! Her sophisticated surgeon husband, a gay junior league bartender, and a drag queen! His biggest fear was getting caught, and yet, so very often, he wished that he would. At least then all the lies would stop and the truth would be out. Regretfully, he was far too weak to face the music and placed all of his energy instead into maintaining the charade. One which he would continue to live secretly for five years more.

In the spring of 2010, it was Peter who would have to tell Anthony about the tragic blood test results that would be sent for re-evaluation to three separate labs throughout the country, at his insistence. It would be Peter who would break down into a fit of rage and despair soon after, that would cause him to drive his Mercedes onto an interstate median, whereby losing control. He would have never told Hannah the truth about why. About how he had been driving and crying and praying—cursing ruefully to God at the moment that he swerved into the far left lane and into oncoming traffic. No, he would not tell her that. Instead, he would only say that he was exhausted and disoriented from lack of sleep. *So what if he ended it all?* he would think, just moments before everything went black. What would it matter? He was a freak and a failure and probably deserved no less. The worst part would be waking up dead inside his heart, strapped to a bed in traction, in his own hospital, and with three cracked ribs and a fractured septum. Nothing would compare to the pain of not being able to see or contact Anthony, who would not even find out about Peter's accident until weeks later. Right before Anthony would go into confinement himself for treatment for the AIDS. He, in all of his goodness, had never wanted Peter to see it. None of it.

Hannah had moved heaven, earth, and her show schedule to dutifully be by her husband's side after his accident. The radio station graciously allowed her to tape several weeks of shows in advance of airing them, whereby granting her a brief leave of absence.

Hannah felt compassion for her overworked surgeon husband, and even blamed herself for any contribution that her busy schedule might have added to his distant and brooding disposition. She'd believed that when he had recovered and started working and traveling again, that things would get better between them. But little did she know that the worst was yet to come.

In less than three months' time, Peter's body was completely healed, but the seams of his and Hannah's marriage were splitting further apart. Peter spent more and more time traveling, primarily to Pennsylvania on *business*, or flying off somewhere with Olivia, causing her to miss school.

Hannah continued to commute weekly to the New York radio station, where she broadcasted her show, taped promos, attended industry events, spoke at luncheons, and met with select private clients "around the fringes." When she was not being America's Dr. Hannah, she was working on writing another self-help book, and working hard at being the best mother possible, and being there for Olivia, her grown sons, and her two granddaughters.

The day that her daughter-in-law, Sara, gave birth to the girls was a joy that she could not explain. Being a grandmother at fifty-five seemed almost as surreal as having a ten-year-old daughter, but in Hannah's mind, it just meant that she and Peter *must* have done something right; that both of their parents had done everything right. It broke her heart, though, that Robert never got to see his great-granddaughters, Emily and Addison, on this Earth and would have to settle for watching them grow up from heaven. Charlotte, whose mind was rapidly declining, would not be able to know that the incredible gift of the two beautiful babies placed in her lap for a holiday photo, were her legacy.

Hannah's family needed her. They all still needed her. There was homework, graduations, courtships, weddings, and so much more to come. Nothing and no one was ever going to change that. She'd only wished all that time that her estranged and increasingly emotionally distant husband felt the same.

Instead, he continued to choose to live a lie.

CHAPTER 25
★ ★ ★

2005

LINDSEY LENNAR WAS A NATURAL beauty. She had moved to New York after her senior year with her mother, to pursue a modeling career, and eventually signed on with the teen division of a prestigious modeling agency. Marney had hired the girl prior to that for several client photo shoots, when she was just getting started with her own agency. But today, it was Lindsey's kid sister, Jaden, Marney was interested in. She'd remembered that Lindsey hailed from none other than Cuyahoga Falls, and that, with a little quick digging, unearthed a workable connection between the Lennar family and Hannah Courtland-Murphy.

There was no doubt that Lindsey, by far, was the beauty in the family, with Carmen Electra-blue eyes, a full mane of golden hair, and a fiercely confident runway walk that teetered between romantic and hard-edged, making her mark on the fashion scene with her doll-like stare. Luckily for Marney, Lindsey's younger sister, Jaden, a gangly sixteen-year-old with jagged braids, crooked teeth, and zero fashion sense, had decided to stay on and attend college locally in Ohio, far from her sister's conspicuous spotlight, to pursue interests of her own. A simple call one day to Lindsey to congratulate her on her latest Calvin Klein billboard sparked a conversation that revealed pay dirt: Lindsey's sister, Jaden, was enrolled in community college and working as a backup babysitter for none other than Hannah Courtland-Murphy. It was fate! Jaden was filling in on weekends to give the Murphys' nanny the needed time off, keeping Jaden in Britney Spears CDs and gas money while she commuted to campus.

Marney was ecstatic and knew just what to do. She now had a use for the other Lennar sister that was about to more than pay off.

Marney contacted Jaden in Ohio, where she lived with her father and younger brother, and invited the girl to the mall under the guise that she was conducting demographic research for the teen market in the Midwest. She had reminded Jaden that she had worked with her sister in the past, and that there would be two concert tickets in it for her if they could simply chat. Why her sister's New York-based former agent wanted to talk with *her* in particular was curious to Jaden, but she welcomed the free tickets and the uncommon attention just the same. After the appropriate amount of time browsing the chain stores, "hanging out" and fostering of trust, Marney went in for the kill once they sat down in the food court. "Your sister tells me that you babysit for the radio show host Dr. Hannah's toddler from time to time."

"Uh-huh" Jaden nodded, about to tear into a messy mall burrito. "I started watching Olivia after school back when Mrs. Murphy was seeing patients at her house. Now it's mostly just on weekends. Her little girl is so cute. You should see her!"

"Really?" Marney slurped the grape-flavored icy drink through a straw that matched her violet eyeliner.

"Yeah, she's really nice, you know—Mrs. Murphy. For a celebrity, I guess." Jaden, attempting to sound unfazed by the fact, meant to sound casual about it all. "Her show is called 'Ask Dr. Hannah,' or something like that. Anyway, everyone's sure that she's going to be famous—like Oprah. She's really awesome."

"Is that so? Has Mrs. Murphy *said* that she's going to be on another radio station?"

"Not exactly. She just sort of told me about how pleased her boss was with the number of listeners she has that last time she drove me home. Hey, maybe you should talk to her about becoming her agent. I don't think she even has one yet."

Music to Marney's ears! Jaden was proving to be quite helpful after all. She pressed the teenager further. "Where does Mrs. Murphy like to hang out? The gym? Supermarket? Any private clubs?"

"Well, she sometimes volunteers at the women's shelter downtown before her show. Sometimes she goes to yoga. I take Olivia to her tumbling class on Saturdays. I stay and watch her, then we walk back to the house. Hannah calls it her 'trampoline time'—whatever that means. She says it's when she catches up on her reading and stuff. Oh, and she has lunch at Victor's Deli every Wednesday before a client session at the clinic. I watch Olivia then, if the nanny is not available."

"I see. Thanks for the information. Maybe I'll give Mrs. Murphy a call and see if she is in need of an agent. I've enjoyed spending the afternoon talking. Have you ever given any thought to doing some headshots yourself?" Marney said, trying to sound complimentary. "I've got a great guy who's a wizard with the teen market. He took your sister's first composite photos, I believe, back when."

Jaden smiled and shook her head. She was all teeth and gums, a gawky bean pole with straight brown hair and a bashful smile, forced to live in the shadow of her fairy-tale princess sister, Lindsey, who held court with modeling agents, star photographers, and designers in her spare time.

"No, thanks. But that is not what you came all this way to ask me, was it?" Jaden opined.

Marney nervously smiled and then produced two tickets to Prince's show at the Grand Arena and handed them to Jaden.

"Wow! Thank you. This is so amazing." Then she paused. "Are you gonna go get her, then? Mrs. Murphy, I mean," Jaden asked shoving the tickets into her jeans pocket.

"You bet your little red corvette, I am. They don't call me the 'Deal Maker' for nothing!"

"They call you that?" Jaden smiled through her braces.

"Just finish your smoothie" Marney chuckled.

CHAPTER 26

★ ★ ★

2005

M ARNEY SCANNED THE RESTAURANT, MOST likely looking for a prima donna radio host with horn-rimmed glasses and a tightly wound chignon. Instead, she found Hannah, a beautiful cherub-faced honey-blonde with sunglasses perched on top of her head, pulling her pageboy neatly behind her ears, revealing tiny diamond stud earrings. She was wearing a Talbot's cashmere sweater top and matching cardigan in periwinkle, a gold wedding band, and a brown leather-band Cartier watch. She was tucked away in a quiet corner booth with her designer pumps off, bending intently over a children's book. It was Dr. Seuss's *Horton Hatches the Egg.* It was research, and one of her guilty pleasures. Every other Friday, Hannah volunteered to lead story time at Olivia's kinder care.

Marney smiled to herself when she approached the table, and Hannah instantly mistook her for the waitress. Without even lifting her gaze from the book, Hannah asked for another cup of tea. "More lemon, too, please."

"Uh, sorry, Doc, I don't wait tables—anymore. Those days are well behind me, I do hope."

Startled, Hannah looked up, regarding the bizarre crea-
ture in a lavender mohair coat standing beside the table.
Her hair was the color of cherry Kool-Aid.

"Pleased to meet you. My name is Marney Valentine, and
I am your new personal agent." Marney peered at her
soon-to-be client over the rims of her rhinestone designer
shades. "And, yes, you can have all the lemons that you
want. I am hell bent and determined to assist in making
you a very rich woman!"

She cracked her pink chewing gum and offered Hannah
a fuchsia-gloved handshake over the deli sandwich on her
plate. "It's really, really good to meet you. I've never repre-
sented a woman shrink before, but then, there's a first time
for everything, right? Great book. I simply *adore* Dr. Seuss."

It was all Hannah could do to smile while her mind was
reeling. *Who was this nutcase? Did she know her from somewhere?* Could she be a crazed fan, or just someone who had
her confused with somebody else?

"My *what*? I don't recall hiring you, Miss. Or anyone
else, for that matter, as my personal anything."

"Yet," Marney corrected her, blowing a messy pink bubble that exploded onto her Kewpie Doll lips.

Hannah intoned calmly. "I do not need a personal agent,
but thank you anyway."

Marney was unfazed by the brush-off. "I thought you
might say that, so I came prepared. Who's representing
you?"

Hannah knew not why, but she played along, "William
Morris. I'm happy with them. Very happy." *Who was this
woman?* Hannah wondered, beginning to grow bothered
by the intrusion. It was the fifth such incident in the past
month, where somebody wanted to talk to her about representation. Peter said it was a good sign, but she just felt
annoyed by the intrusions. Still, in spite of this, the strange
woman intrigued her. She was relentless, yet impressively
confident, and there was something vaguely familiar about

her East Coast accent.

Suddenly, Hannah remembered a string of phone calls over the past few weeks that had dogged her—at the reception desk at the station, on her voice mail, on her private line at home. She had meant to return her calls and say "no, thanks," but she had just been too busy.

"I brought my portfolio," Marney said plopping a large lizard-print leather binder on the table. "May I—?"

Hannah bit her lip and shrugged. As if she could even hope to stop her.

Marney slid into the chair across from the small table and was now officially "at lunch" with *the* Dr. Hannah. Together, they walked through the contents of the binder. Company names on letterhead that meant little or nothing to Hannah. She smiled politely as Marney expounded on her professional prowess in landing such "prestigious" and fortunate clients as these with her stunning representation.

In a fatal, mood-altering moment of flailing disinterest, Marney jumped in for the save.

"But you're not interested in what I've done for all my other clients, am I right? Of course not. You're interested in what I can do for *you*."

Hannah smiled placidly. She was trapped. A Cyndi Lauper lookalike was trying to sell her a bill of goods. Twenty more minutes before she would be due back at the clinic for her three o'clock standing session. She read her watch. "Do hurry, then. I have an appointment to get to."

Marney impressed Hannah with her knowledge and love for the business in sixty seconds flat. She emphasized the market's need for a magnetic personality who spoke to the masses with solid advice and moral contention. This got Hannah's interest, and she piped in. "Then you *get* what I'm trying to do? You see, ninety-five percent of the population is aware of the right thing to do when they're stuck between a hard place and their wavering egos. Frankly, I believe that we humans know the difference and know the solutions. It's elementary. It's just that—"

"Sometimes we all just need a good swift kick in the ass?" Marney said.

Hannah slammed the table, just missing her fork. "Yes! Yes, yes, and quadruple—yes!"

Marney leaned in on her elbows. "I say that there's a bigger market for the wisdom and insights of the great Dr. Hannah Courtland-Murphy, and I don't mean a second-rate radio station in Ohio. The choice is really yours, Hannah. Is William Morris going to give you the kind of attention and promote you with the kind of effort it takes to cultivate a sensation? Because I see sensation, Hannah. Isn't that what we're talking about here? Moving mountains? Changing people, fixing lives—right? One caller at a time."

Hannah smiled, seeing the possibilities.

"I'm good at what I do. It's as simple as that," Marney professed. "You won't get a lot of bullshit from me. I'm a straight shooter with a head for business, a heart for fairness, and a gut for knowing what to do. I'll go to the mat for you; do whatever it takes to maximize your potential. I believe in transparency. True partnership and trust."

Hannah wondered to herself. Would she ever be able to trust someone with her future? Should she even do so? What about her family? She had trusted Peter to always know what to do, and he was failing her—failing all of them.

Marney held out a peacock blue business card with her name scripted in luxurious swirls on the front in the kitschiest shade of orange paprika. "Take it. I'm certain that I could help you get to where ever it is you're heading. It's up to you, of course." Then, craftily quoting the master himself, she tapped the children's book that Hannah had been reading and said, "*I meant what I said, and I said what I meant. An elephant's faithful, one hundred per cent!*"

She placed the garish card on the table, leaving Hannah

sitting there just as she had found her. Then she turned on her heel and clicked off, not looking back, her voice trailing, "Call me!"

Bewildered, Hannah studied the business card, wondering, much to her chagrin, if a character like Marney could possibly get her to her dreams, her goals, to the place where she was heading. Who knew? She, for one, did not.

CHAPTER 27
★ ★ ★

HANNAH TOSSED HER KEYS ONTO the kitchen counter, along with two parcels from the local grocery in tow. She fixed herself, the sitter, and the kids a healthy dinner of lemon chicken breast and vegetables, leaving Peter's on the counter wrapped in foil. She paid a few utility bills, checked in with the nursing home, listened to the phone calls blinking on the archaic office answering machine, read Olivia a story, and then put her to bed. She took a quick shower and got ready to turn in herself.

That night, she dreamt of a job that paid more. A four-hour show taped in two; freedom to see only choice clients, more book sales, a promotional tour. She envisioned a whir of contracts, syndication, royalties; the rest of the kids' colleges paid in full; a summer home, the Safe Haven Shelter project realized, more time with Peter to fix their marriage—and early retirement. Marney's words resounded in her head as she finally drifted off to sleep. *"I'm certain that I could help you get to where ever it is you're heading. It's up to you."*

She knew first-hand how difficult it had been to try and self-promote herself along with all of her other responsibilities in hope of reaching a larger audience—and thus playing in a bigger market. Breaking through on talent alone was not enough. She lamented the times when she would practically have to beg someone to listen to her sound reel, or read her poorly produced press packet that she had put together with her word processing program. More often than not, at age fifty, she was not even given a fair chance. One stodgy executive from a Canadian-based broadcasting company even went so far as to insult her when she shook hands with him at a charity event and offered to send him a media kit. He was not a fan of her take-no-prisoner's tactics and straight-from-the-hip advice, brushing her off briskly. He even went so far as to mock her in esteemed company, saying, *"Who is really going to want to take advice from a nagging housewife?"* What she needed was credibility, and that could only come from taking the leap to the next level and securing exclusive representation.

By the time she awoke to greet the day, she had already decided to give Marney a try. She would let her see if she could negotiate a solid deal with the radio station on *her* terms, or find something better. The alarm on the bureau sprang on full tilt at seven a.m., blaring the peppy WCLK wake-up morning jingle—right on cue. There were Kip and Sidney broadcasting their same tired shtick to the same tired audience. That would be her fate if she just settled for the status quo and allowed the station to keep her held down when there was a bigger world out there to reach.

Hannah smiled. It was a sign. She grabbed the cordless phone from the nightstand and dialed the number Marney had given her. "Congratulations, Ms. Valentine. You've got yourself a new client. Let's do this!"

CHAPTER 28
★ ★ ★

"SO THIS IS IT," HANNAH said, pulling the Mercedes into the narrow parking spot located next to two dumpsters at the Cuyahoga Falls Community Center near the back entrance. "You said that you wanted to see where I learned how to do what I do."

Marney paused to take it all in. The exterior looked like any other public city building with a weathered brick façade and postage-stamp-size windows with security bars and a chain gate that had left scrapes across the asphalt from years of use.

"This is where the volunteers go in. It's closest to the back offices. I'll show you." Hannah grabbed her Prada handbag and shoved it beneath the leather seat. Marney took notice and did the same. "No need to put on airs," Hannah said. It was one of the many things that Marney admired most about her new client. Hannah was her best self when she was just an ordinary citizen, not a celebrity, reaching out to others in need. This was a great opportunity for Hannah to show Marney where she had come from; to revisit her early days as a volunteer therapist at the clinic where she'd honed her craft and made lasting connections. It was paramount that she got to know Hannah—everything about her—and as quickly as possible.

The two walked around to the double steel doors just as an older man was leaving. They slipped into the quiet hall, Marney close on Hannah's heels as they walked past several small rooms, where therapists were conducting sessions. "We'll go to the main lobby first, and then I'll show you around." Hannah's calming presence was evident in the hesitant glances from the solemn faces that approached and passed them in the halls. Hannah greeted each person with eye contact and a wide smile. "Good morning!" and "How are you today?" was offered to each and every passerby. There was a sullen teen girl with skeletal arms poking through a tank top and piercings along her earlobes, nose, and lip whose eyes averted when they passed.

"This way" Hannah pulled to the right, and, together, they rounded a corner of a small waiting area comprised of one well-worn couch and several tattered chairs. "This is where the clients would wait for their session with a counselor." Marney nodded, taking in the gravity of it all and feeling the pulse of the room, which was strangely silent, even though every chair was filled with a waiting occupant. One man had brought a paper sack that he kept checking and folding on his lap as an ancient, gray-whiskered mutt curled contented at his feet.

"Hi, Betty!" Hannah said, addressing the middle-aged woman seated behind the reception desk. "This is my friend Marney. We're here for a little tour today."

The woman smiled and stood to give Hannah a hug. "Haven't seen you in such a long while, but"—she lowered her voice to a nicotine-infused whisper—"I listen to your show every afternoon on my way home."

Hannah smiled. She had definitely come a long way,

and returning to the place of her early days working with the community really hit a chord with her as well. "I'm delighted to be back here. Nothing has changed."

The woman threw a knowing glance toward Hannah's colorful companion, who was eyeing a jar of tiny lollipops. "Oh, I wouldn't exactly say *that.*" She snickered. And then, to Marney: "Help yourself, dear."

"Thank you." Marney smiled. "I had to come see Hannah's old stomping grounds. You do good work here."

Together, they walked through a series of several more carpeted halls and finally stopped at a door with a sign dangling from the doorknob that read: *Session in Progress.* "This was my office," Hannah said wistfully. "At least, it was mostly where I saw clients when I volunteered here on and off through the years. I even brought Olivia here in her bouncy chair. There is a nursery just down the hall. Let me show you."

They walked farther along the worn carpet to a set of double glass doors. The smell of glue and curdled milk hit Marney hard when they stepped inside. A Hispanic woman was holding an infant in her arms, and a toddler was drooling happily on all fours. Hannah shook her head. "Brings back memories, all right."

"So, you would bring Olivia along with you to work?" Marney said, trying to picture Hannah juggling responsibilities just to help others.

"Some days I would bring her; other times, leave her with a sitter. I remember, in particular, when I realized how much of a refuge this place was for so many people. It was that *one* day, no one will forget. It started like any other Tuesday. I had headed in here to sign some paperwork before making my nine fifteen a.m. yoga class. I had the Lennar girl sitting for Olivia just until noon so I could knock out a few errands following the class just before heading home for my one o'clock client. When I entered the office at eight fifty-five, the waiting room here was abuzz with the news of a plane crash into the North Tower of the World Trade Center in New York."

Marney nodded. Who *didn't* remember where they were standing at that exact minute? It was etched in every person's brain with acuity.

"Something very bad had just happened, the center's director said, gathering the staff into the kitchenette for an emergency meeting. 'I'm going to need all hands on deck. This is going to cause a lot of anxiety and confusion—people are going to need us; to talk to someone.' She turned to me directly and said, 'Can you stay?' Of course I said that I could stay up until noon, and that I would then make arrangements to come back—for as long as they would need me. Little did anyone know what would follow.

"I worked all morning on the phone lines in my yoga tights and leotard, and then the next two weeks straight was a blur of double shifts, extra private counseling sessions, and evenings watching 24/7 coverage of the news that changed history before everyone's eyes. People wondered: *Was the world coming to an end? Had the worst come?* These were the questions that everyone was asking. It was so tense."

"That must have been rough. I mean, who knew those answers, right?" Marney said as they turned and headed toward the break room.

"'Why did they do this to us?' Broderick had asked me one evening at dinner. It was just he, Olivia, and me at the kitchen table. Peter was pulling all-nighters in the ER and was talking about going to Ground Zero to offer medical assistance where needed. The house was otherwise empty except for the constant glow of the television permanently broadcasting the events sans the sound. I said that I didn't know, but that it had a lot of people worried," Hannah said in a serious tone. "What killed me the most was that did little to cull his fourteen-year-old fears. 'I don't want Dad to go there!' he had said, slamming his fork onto the plate and storming out of the room. I thought, *If I can't comfort my own son, how in the world can I ever hope to help others?* It really rattled me, back then."

Marney nodded knowingly. "But how could you have blamed him? How could you have blamed anyone for feeling so afraid and confused at that time?"

"That's the thing with this gig. You never really know *if* you have helped. Not always.

"I just vowed then and there that I would need to do better in making my children feel safe—

no matter what. That my family would come first. That's all that anyone really wants, I think, in life—to take care of the of the ones they love."

"How did you manage to take all that on, plus *this*?" Marney asked as they settled onto two plastic chairs at a rickety table near a noisy vending machine in the far end of the break room.

Hannah smiled. "I don't know. Sometimes it was rough. I guess I just didn't think about it, I just did what I had to do to be there for those people who needed someone to talk to. Many nights it was just me and a few other volunteers on the crisis line, answering calls for hours."

"How was that experience?" Marney asked, tearing into a bag of Bugles scored for four quarters, two dimes, and a nickel from the vending machine. "I mean, were you really able to talk someone down from ending it all?"

"Sometimes. Yes—pretty often. It might have been a long conversation, but eventually, we could usually talk them down. I remember one young man who was so distraught about losing his job that he agreed to meet with me after I promised that I would work with him in our database to find him some temporary employment for the short term. I had to *bribe* him to come in to the office. He was waffling, and I feared that he would not show up the next day."

"So, what did you do?"

"I offered to bring him lunch. I asked, 'So, what do you like on your sandwich? Mustard, or mayo?' I remember going over the details of this lunch with him so that he would feel obligated to show up. So that I could keep him from contemplating suicide for another twenty-four hours. Hoping that the urge would pass until I could talk with him face-to-face."

"Did it work?" Marney said expectantly.

"It did. For him, but it didn't always work. That was the sad part." Hannah's voice trailed as she glanced around the room, suddenly feeling strangely detached, it seemed, from the world that taught her to be *Dr. Hannah*. In so many ways, the moment felt surreal. "Once, we lost a young man who was just seventeen. He had his whole life ahead of him, and he threw it all away over a broken heart. Some, you just have to accept that you can't save," Hannah said.

"What was the weirdest client experience you ever had as a therapist?" Marney asked, hoping to change the mood. "Anything funny ever go down?"

Hannah thought and then chuckled. "It was years later, in my clinical practice when I was working here on weekends and I counseled a family where the father had been incarcerated and the mother had recently passed away. A foster family was raising the young boy. He was really sweet and smart, but he had just stopped speaking. They came in with this issue, and the foster mother was desperate for services. We placed the boy with a speech therapist, and I worked with him intensively to help him through the abandonment issues. Eventually, he gained back his self-esteem and began opening up. He started communicating and showed great promise that delighted him and his foster family. He returned to thank me one day. I'll never forget how he gave me a shoe box wrapped with a piece of string. It felt like it had a tiny rock or stone in it when I shook it. He told me that it was something that he had made for me."

"How sweet" Marney smiled.

"No—wait. When I opened it right there in front of him, do you know what I found in that box as his *gift* that he made?"

"Oh no—" Marney winced as she read Hannah's face.

"It was a piece of feces. It was what he had 'made' for me, wrapped up in that box!"

"Oh *shit!*" Marney howled.

"Exactly!" Hannah said, shaking her head at the memory. "It doesn't get more real than that!"

Next, they headed to the radio station at WLCK, where Hannah proudly gave Marney the grand tour of the fish-bowl glass lobby, sales offices, and the two recording studios glowing with blinking lights. It was still early in the day, and Kip and Sidney had just signed off. Hannah high-fived Sidney as they passed by a line of neatly arranged cubicles just off the executive offices to her own little corner of the world—a tiny back office about the size of a broom closet, but with a stunning view of the city through a large double-pane window displaying the city skyline.

"Wow! Not too shabby," Marney said, fondling the goods like a grabby pop-up-sale shopper. Hannah had a pricey leather chair, a narrow vintage bookcase, and bronze-plated awards tacked to the boring gray walls. In the corner, there was a single potted plant.

"It's home away from home" Hannah smiled. "I'm happy here."

"Are you?" Marney broached, ever the sales person and eager agent keen on pushing the envelope. "I say that we can do *better* than this."

Hannah shook her head pensively, her eyes sweeping across the corner of her desk, where her life was displayed in a myriad of framed photos, mementos, and crayon drawings. And then she smiled. "That's why I hired you!"

The next several months were a blur of activity. Marney was relentless with requests for show tapings, publicity photos, and pushes for Hannah to do more promotions than ever. She booked her for every woman's interest and mental health trade show, grand opening, and product endorsement opportunity that even remotely worked to get her name and brand out into the world front and center. She revamped Hannah's website and sharpened her media kit to include public speaking engagements, seminars, and even an online advice blog that eventually became the basis for three self-help books to follow. No stone was left unturned as Marney made it her life and passion to bring Hannah's unique style and star-power into the limelight—and ultimately, to a bigger audience.

CHAPTER 29
★ ★ ★

IT WASN'T LONG BEFORE LIFE began to change
in ways that Hannah had never imagined. Once large
billboards with her smiling face appeared on interstate
roadsides, park benches, and bus sides, touting her radio
show on WCLK's "big 89-AM" mid-mornings from 10:00
a.m. to 2:00 p.m., she became a mainstay for commut-
ers and listeners looking for hard-and-fast advice. It was
Marney's idea to promote the "real woman" behind the
credentials. One catchy slogan read: *This Mom Wears Jeans
and Has the Answers!* Making Hannah personable also had
the unintended effect of causing the public to feel like they
knew her. This made living her daily life nothing short of
impossible some days.

It was nothing for Hannah to be recognized in public,
which, flattering as it was, sometimes caused distress when
a dinner out with her kids got interrupted by a gushing
fan, or a nail appointment turned into a free advice-fest
as she was made to field questions from manicurists and
patrons of every new salon she tried to slip away to. Ano-
nymity was a right that she had forfeited in exchange for
more listeners, more clicks on her website, and more brand
reach.

"People are staring," Broderick said one pizza night at the mall. "Those women over there are pointing and freaking out."

"Try to ignore them. I do," Hannah said, dabbing Olivia's face with a wet wipe. "It comes with the territory, right?" Then she laughed. "Don't complain when it's helping to send you to college."

He smirked. "You got a point there."

Ever since Broderick could remember, his mother was there for *someone*. That's what he loved about her most. Seeing her image on a billboard meant nothing new, because he had always had the real thing, and the woman up there was just a cardboard face in the clouds. Still, though, it was pretty cool sometimes when being the child of Dr. Hannah scored them free access to events, and sometimes even righteous swag from stores and restaurants. As far as Broderick was concerned, celebrity had its perks. That's why he was dead-set on attending Arizona State University in the fall on a golf scholarship and minoring in sports management. If he could not be a pro himself in the game, he would definitely like to manage a string of great careers in the sport.

"What is happening with prom?" Hannah asked casually. Getting a straight answer out of her loving son was like pulling teeth sometimes. "Have you asked Penny Swist yet? She really is a sweet girl. Her mother and I work the fundraiser every year for the school. Her parents are lovely."

"Yeah, I asked her."

"Well? Did she say yes?" Hannah pressed.

"She said yes." He reddened at bit, downplaying the whole thing. Much like Peter, he was not one to gush about anything.

"Of course she said yes!" Hannah smiled.

"I did a promposal that was pretty low-key, but she loved it. I had the Starbucks girl write, *Will You Go To Prom With Me?* with the Sharpie on Penny's latte and waited for her to catch on. She squealed and starting posting photos of it everywhere. I think she dug it."

"Great!" Hannah said. "We will have two events to celebrate that night—your prom and Olivia's spring pageant. Your father and I are going to divide and conquer. I will be seeing you and Penny off for the evening around six p.m., after I attend a quick station appearance, while your father will be attending Olivia's debut as one of the three princesses in *The Frog and the Princess* at her preschool earlier at five thirty p.m."

It was not uncommon for many of the milestones in the Murphy family to be split between the thirteen-year time span between Broderick and Olivia's ages. It was never boring, that was for sure.

However, when the big day came for each of them, Peter was once again called out of town, leaving Hannah with a quandary. How would she be able to pull off *both* events? It simply was not possible for her to attend both at the same time. Much to her delight and relief, Broderick stepped up in a way that left even his loquacious mother speechless. He and Penny talked it over and decided to forego their dinner date before the actual prom and accompany Olivia themselves.

"We've got this, Mom," Broderick had said, opting instead, to use the limo he had rented for the evening to transport his lovely date, Penny, *and* his adorable princess little sister to the pageant. They must have been a sight, Hannah had thought to herself, her handsome, kind, loving son escorting a five-year-old on one arm and his beautiful teen prom date on the other, sitting in formal attire, with boutonniere and corsage in the tiny plastic chairs of Olivia's kinder-care classroom.

Broderick and Penny arrived back to the house at eight o'clock to return Olivia, who was carrying a small bouquet of pink roses after having the adventure of her life.

"Look, Mommy—everyone took our picture!"

The shots of the night went viral, taken from parents and attendees of the pageant, and then later, when Dr. Hannah Courtland-Murphy's son and his date rolled up to the prom late, making a grand entrance. Everyone who had seen the pictures on social media applauded and cheered when they walked into the banquet hall.

Hannah held her daughter a bit closer that night when she tucked her in. "You have quite the big brother there, don't you?" she had said to her sleepy-eyed daughter, who yawned and smiled. She still had the diamond tiara next to her on the pillow.

"Did I ever tell you about your Grandma Charlotte and your Grandpa Robert and the way they met in a fairy tale many years ago?"

Olivia nodded, but asked her to tell it again. It was the perfect ending to the perfect of days.

CHAPTER 30
★ ★ ★

2006

THANKS TO MARNEY'S TENACITY AND the public's voracious appetite for Hannah's addictive appeal, the first business day of the New Year, Hannah signed a five-year syndication deal with WCLK's parent company, Venture Media Network in New York. The company had investments in several major market radio stations, a twenty-four-hour all-talk radio behemoth franchise; a cable sports network, and over two hundred fifty Internet and satellite radio channels. Arrangements were made for her to commute four days a week on a six a.m. commercial airline to JFK Airport, where a car would be waiting to take her to the Manhattan studio.

Hannah had made the initial trip to meet with the network solo, as Peter was too swamped at the hospital to steal away for even two days to accompany his wife in New York City for the formal interview. No surprise. So Hannah went alone. She treated herself to a new little black dress from Bloomingdale's, a symphony, and ultimately, a career move that would, hopefully, solidify her place in broadcasting history.

The offices of Venture Media had been much bigger, and certainly more intimidating than Hannah had imagined, filled with busy, dedicated professionals, mostly young, single types with high-end cars, expensive coffee drinks, and upper east-side walk-up co-ops, she'd supposed.

A feeling of "high expectation" hung in the air, causing a prominent elevation to the task for which Hannah was once quite comfortable with. This was serious business, and for the first time ever, as she stood in the mammoth glass showcase corner office of the station's general manager, Allison Michaels, awaiting her interview, she secretly questioned her right to be there.

"Remember," Marney had coached just twelve weeks earlier as she spun Hannah around in the stylist's chair, "you want to look as bad-ass and fierce as your advice, so we're going *blonder*—bolder." Then, turning to the colorist, "Don't be afraid to up the wattage here. I want Gwen Stefani meets Hillary Clinton."

The haircut and color were just the beginning of Marney's master makeover plan. She promptly placed Hannah on a plant-based diet and a punishing five-day-a-week workout regimen, proselytizing, "You can't be beautiful if you don't feel beautiful, so let's get to it!"

She had hired a personal trainer and soon interval weight training, Pilates, and kickboxing were added to Hannah's overbooked schedule. Marney even put a stationary bicycle in her home office, commanding her to "log as many miles as you can in between clients."

The pace was grueling, but after just five weeks, Hannah had never felt better or looked more ready for prime time. It was mind over matter, and having someone with Marney's determination and gusto was just the kick in the behind that Hannah, and her career, needed. She was only a psychotherapist from Ohio with a successful local radio show, with two children still living at home. She had a four-bedroom mid-century brick home, a Chevy Caravan, a couple of dogs, a mortgage, and a garden of begonias badly in need of pruning, but she had a persona and a set of gams that could turn heads. She was ready to tackle the world. When it was all said and done, and thanks to Marney's shrewd negotiations with the network, Dr. Hannah Courtland-Murphy agreed to sign on and join the Venture Media family with her afternoon radio show that would be blasted on over thirty-five stations nationwide.

CHAPTER 31
★ ★ ★

2009

PETER'S LIFE HAD BECOME A web of lies, a carefully planned balancing act between work, home, and his alternative life with Anthony, stowed away in Philadelphia along with a second set of clothes, an additional bank account, and a new group of friends. Although he walked a fine line between two worlds, it was his family back in Cuyahoga Falls from which he withheld the truth and caused the most consternation. It was not uncommon for him to miss a big event, such as a prom, graduation, or engagement party, or a move to a new home for his eldest, as a result of commitments he had made to Anthony, which more often than not, took precedence, especially once Anthony's diagnosis was made clear and every minute spent with him would prove to be precious and unretractable.

It was not easy for Peter to bounce between two worlds and to conceal the parts of him that felt the most real, the most authentic. Peter never really reveled in Hannah's newfound success, or even in his own. He felt so fragmented that he often wondered if he ever really was giving his "all" to any of his loved ones. In many ways he was a fraud, and the thought haunted and tormented him when he stood still long enough to feel the guilt creep into his mind or take a hold of his anxieties and manifest in full-blown panic attacks and searing blows to his gut whenever he considered too deeply the situation he had created for himself. Rather than continually berate himself mercilessly, he instead began to turn his anger onto Hannah—his loving and faithful wife, who never deserved to be deceived in such a brutal and hurtful way. But what was he to do? How else could he get up from their bed each time and head out for another flight to Philly and the waiting arms of his best friend and lover? He had once thought that it was Hannah who had all the answers for everyone—for him. But not anymore. The damage had been done.

He even went so far as to seek counseling of his own, confiding in a colleague at the hospital there in Ohio when he was in the throes of his deceptive, duo life.

"Tell me. What brings you here, today?"

"I have hurt a lot of people with my actions," Peter said, instantly regretting his choice of going with a therapist who might recognize him or his high-profile wife. "This is confidential, right?"

"Of course, Dr. Murphy. May I call you, Peter?" she asked, opening her legal pad and untwisting the top of an expensive pen. "Completely confidential."

Peter shifted a bit on the uncomfortable leather couch, pushing a decorative pillow into his lower back nervously. The room smelled like lavender and vanilla, not unlike Hannah's side of the bathroom sink.

"Why don't you tell me what you mean by, 'hurt a lot of people'?" she said.

He thought that she looked no older than Marc, his second eldest, who had just started a job on the West Coast with a start-up tech company. *What could she know about this sort of thing?* Would it be any less absurd than calling in anonymously to a radio shrink like Hannah? Then he checked his errant thoughts quickly—thinking himself to be insensitive. *See?* he thought disgustedly. He couldn't help himself.

"I am married to a wonderful woman. I have three grown sons and a nine-year-old daughter. And I'm gay."

If this startled the junior-league therapist, she didn't show it, except for a slightly raised eyebrow above her Gucci frames.

"I see," she said. And then faced him squarely. "Is your family aware of this?"

He lowered his head and began to cry. "I am betraying them in every way . . . every day."

"It's all right to talk here. This is a safe place," she said, handing him a box of tissues. "What are you hoping for here?"

"I don't know."

Silence as he wiped his eyes.

Finally, she volleyed a barrage of questions. "Are you sleeping?"

"Yes."

"Are you eating?"

"Yes."

"Are you thinking of hurting yourself?"

"No, I-I just want to know what to do!" he exploded. "I am seeing someone, another man in another city, and I have a wife and family here. I'm conflicted. I don't know who I am half the time."

"Do you want to end the relationship?"

"Which one?"

"Either one? With him, or your marriage? Peter, do you think that you can have both?"

"I-I don't know. I suppose I can't, or shouldn't. I just don't have it all figured out yet."

"Do you want to? Figure it out, I mean?" she asked

plainly and without judgment.

He looked at her striking eyes and cascading dark hair that fell past her shoulders just above her full breasts. She was a beautiful woman. An attractive, sensual, heterosexual woman, yet he didn't desire her in any way. He was completely and irrevocable homosexual. He was in love with Anthony.

And with that realization, he had his answer. "I don't need to figure out who I am, or what I want. I just have to find the strength to own it. The truth is, I can't. Not now, at least."

"Why don't we make an appointment for you to come see me once a week to help you sort out these feelings?" she said, scribbling the date five days from then on a business card. He took the offering and nodded. Then he grabbed his jacket and sidled out the door into the hall.

When the elevator descended to the lobby and the doors popped open, he pitched the appointment card into a trash receptacle and strode out of the revolving door, back to his duplicitous life.

CHAPTER 32
★ ★ ★

2006

THE WEEK AFTER SEALING THE deal, Hannah and
Marney met with the network executives for lunch at
The Palm to celebrate the signing on of Hannah with Venture Media Network. Allison brought along Jon Novotny,
who would be Hannah's producer—if he met with her
approval. He was a twenty-something hot shot from Lan-
sing, Michigan, who had done wonders for his career by
sleeping with Allison back in 1996, when she was still bedding boys whose careers she could advance in exchange
for sexual favors. She was then-station manager of WDTR
in Detroit, and he was a hopeful graduate looking for a
break. He got one, all right. Allison hired him on the board
and as an assistant to the producer of the *Gregg & Gary
Romus Show*, and within two years' time, was solely producing Gregg and Gary's irreverent garbage hate-fest on
Detroit's "Big Thirty-Nine."

When the show went syndicate, Novotny was sent out
west to Phoenix with the incorrigible Gregg and Gary
team, whose propensity for trash talk and wild stunt-radio
antics took the industry by storm. They were overnight

sensations among males twenty-five to fifty-four years old,
eventually fouling the airwaves on twenty-seven stations
from Hollywood to Hometown USA with their special
brand of "blue humor." As it turned out, the Romuses
were not actually brothers at all—far from it. They were
fraternity brothers from out East who maintained the farce
of their being siblings into their act.

Contractual legalities and, eventually a bad cocaine habit
shared by both resulted in a quick and devastating decline
of the show's popularity, which was ultimately dropped in
its second year in syndication.

Novotny then returned to the Midwest with resume in
hand, a little older, far more experienced, and looking for
an entirely different kind of show to produce. A few well-
placed references brought him, once again, across the desk
from Allison Michaels, who was then program director of
WRCK, a classic rock format in Cincinnati. She had a
morning show badly in need of creative witch doctoring.
Jon saw the challenge for what it was—a job no one else
wanted to take—but hungry and determined, he agreed to
produce the segments.

The host was a twenty-two-year-old former rock musician, turned disc jockey who called himself *Spit*. Further,
and more pointedly, he was the son of none other than
veteran shock-jock and Howard Stern clone, Jesse J. James
out of L.A.

Jon was desperate. Spit actually had a knack for the
medium and managed to turn out some very brilliant
content every now and then, which could eventually con-
tribute to the rising success of the ailing station. Allison
had since become a self-proclaimed lesbian with a pretense
for wearing men's boxers underneath her power suits. She
had gained a good thirty pounds, ditched make-up alto-
gether, and wore a men's wristwatch. It was a look that
worked well for her and often garnered respect from a staff
that both feared and loved to hate her.

But what did he care? He didn't need to pork ugly women anymore to score a decent job. *Those days are over,* Jon had decreed. Under his brilliant handiwork producing WRCK's morning show, remarkably, the ratings did grow substantially for the next eighteen months.

Allison was still hell on wheels. She had bigger balls than all of the swinging dicks in the company, and she knew it. She took heat behind her back for being a dyke, but the numbers did not lie. Allison Michaels could deliver the winners in all four day-parts.

Spit-in-the-Morning, along with the brilliant assistance of Jon Novotny, was the golden combination of high-watt wit and wonder, eventually bringing the radio station mainstay positioning as a noted industry leader for eighteen months running.

Eventually, Jon left WRCK in the spring of 2003 to pursue his own company. It was a sound recording business in Akron that failed in two quick years. He had been working odd jobs ever since and was just about to consider going back to producing when he got the call.

Allison was now general manager of radio powerhouse Venture Media Network in New York and was, it would seem, about to influence his life in yet another strange and wonderful way, by calling him out of the blue not eight weeks ago.

"How are things, Jon? Business ever take off?"

"Not exactly."

It was music to her ears. "Still dreaming of getting to the coast someday? I hear that Leo Stecker is looking for a tape-runner. He's looking for someone to produce his DJ-Rapper, a two-ton wonder boy named Enrique, on the midday drive mix in Burbank."

"Are you tossin' me a load of crap, Allison?" Jon had become cynical, to say the least, about the radio business.

"Maybe."

"Well, maybe I really ain't interested in whatever it is you're sellin'. And besides, I love the goddamn winters here too much to even *think* of ever leaving."

"Mmmm . . . is that so? Guess K-Country in Tulsa is definitely not an option either, then?   Cowboy boots included!"

"What are you, *high*? I'd starve before I'd do Country. Hey, isn't it about time you start firing someone's ass over there by now? It's nearly noon, or are you losing your touch?"

"Fire? Hell no! Bro, I'm *adding* bodies, baby. Got a new show that's going to be big. It's already causing a buzz."

"Yeah? Who's the guy?"

"He's a *she.*"

"What? Another New-Age diva? No, don't tell me. A food critic? A cooking queen?"

"Nope. She's a shrink, and you should hear her. She's a stitch. I swear to God, Jonny, you gotta hear her to believe it. I'm sending you some tape. Listen and see what you think."

"Why?"

"Because, my friend, if you're interested, I might be inclined to hire *your* ass to produce her show. What do you say to that?"

"Seriously? A *talk* format? I don't know."

"You're the best guy for the job, Jon, hands down." Her voice unsoftened. "I need you, goddammit! Now listen to the tapes I'm sending you, and then say no—all right?"

"Okay. I'll listen, but I'm not promising anything." *She always has to win.* He chuckled to himself. *Dykes.*

When Allison hung up the phone, she was already commending herself on her victory, thinking the same thing of him. *Producers.*

Jon approached the table five minutes early, as was typical. He was slender and a tad bit older around the eyes than Allison had remembered. Not at all what she had pictured from the phone conversation. He was only nineteen when she had first met him. That was ten years ago. A lot had changed since then, all right.

Now, his once-long hair had receded and was neatly trimmed close at the neck. He looked centered and confident in his indigo blue shirt; oddly settled, in his maturity, wearing starched chinos and comic strip tie. He had come a long way from denim jackets and torn blue jeans, but still had his own style. Jon Novotny was all grown up.

Allison smiled, remembering the early days. What was she thinking back then? She had been with Lisa now for going on six years, and making love with her made more sense than anything Allison had ever known. Even taming the unbridled passions of young virgin innocents like him. She cringed at the thought.

At least she knew her stuff when it came to pairing talent. She was dead certain that seated at the table, that very moment, was a winning combination that she could take to the bank.

"Hannah, this is Jon Novotny. Jon, meet Dr. Hannah Courtland-Murphy."

The two sized each other up in a hot instant. Jon saw a fairly attractive housewife-type, from suburbia no doubt, with a nervous edge tightening around a forced smile. She appeared to be indifferent, but pleased with the young man she would need to trust with the trajectory of her career. Hannah smiled after looking him squarely in the eye, indicating that he would do.

They shook on it. The moment their hands joined, a synergy seemed to flow from one into the other. Later, they would say it was an "instant connection." Allison would say that it was ratings destiny. Either way, no greater team ever existed in a studio before, or ever since. No other professional relationship depended more on trust, chemistry, and talent than that which was about to change the direction of radio—and their lives. Times were changing, and destiny was waiting.

CHAPTER 33

★ ★ ★

2006

BACK HOME, OLIVIA WAS ONLY six, and Hannah hated like hell leaving her so often, but there was little choice.

"I'm a big *gurl* now!" Olivia would sternly tell Hannah. "It's okay if you have to *woirk* in New *Yoirk*, Mommy. I'll be all right."

Hannah would smile and hug her daughter—the most significant miracle of her life, who was fast becoming the most well-adjusted of them all. Her boys were fast embracing young adulthood, and so, holding on to Olivia's childhood was more precious to her than gold. They all wanted their mother to be "Dr. Hannah" for the world, as long as she remained special to them. That was the deal she had made. And the promise she would keep. It did not matter how many tens of thousands of people they shared her with, she would always be their mom, and they knew that they were the light of her life.

Hannah kept dozens of framed photos of her loving family at the New York studio adorning her cubicle, along with promotional shots, vacation post cards, and Olivia's handmade artwork. While everyone often teased her for being a "toughie" with callers, intolerant of sniveling nay-sayers and indecisive self-pleasers, there was a sentimental and truly tender side to Hannah that few colleagues ever saw. For the most part, she kept her private life separate from her work.

One of Hannah's favorite photos was that of her wedding day. It was February 1977, just two days before Valentine's Day. Even though she and Peter had a simple ceremony without family and friends present, it meant no less, as they were two sweethearts ready to take on the world and all life had to bring. Hannah marveled at the many ways that she had changed since those early years. The young woman in the photo wearing a long, gauzy white dress embroidered with daisies matching the flowers in her hair. Her small waist was encircled with bands of ribbon matching the ones flowing from her bell sleeves. She was carefree and hopeful, but in so many ways, naïve. Jumping into marriage and family right away was old-fashioned. It was the safe thing to do. Hannah had always thought of herself, even then, as being independent and somewhat of a pioneer spirit. Still, she had no regrets about the choices she had made. And if she had learned anything in the time that she had been on this earth, it was to be resilient. The best answers came with time, and a good life was made so by experiencing the good with the bad.

Hannah held on to her values, fully knowing that it was one of the only things in life one could count on—that and change.

CHAPTER 34
★ ★ ★

2007

THE TRAGIC NEWS IN THE way of a single phone call that came in the night informing Hannah that her father, Robert, had suffered a heart attack and died in his sleep, ripped the breath from her lungs. It was the height of her professional career unexpectedly crossing paths with the most profound personal loss she could ever imagine. The only blessing being that Charlotte would have no comprehension of the event. The family held a quiet and private service graveside with a color guard send-off befitting of a national hero.

Hannah leaned on Peter, who stood stoic and emotionless, only adding to her enormous grief. The boys, hardy young men, huddled around Olivia, wiping their tears and trying to remain strong through muffled sobs.

"Do you really need to keep checking your phone?" Hannah said as her heels sank into the wet grass, where they all stood graveside in the cool spring breeze. The wind lifted the organza ribbon on her Derby sun hat. Beneath the brim, she concealed her red, swollen eyes with an oversize pair of dark Borghese sunglasses. She looked every bit like a widow instead of the grieving daughter she was, and the irony of it was not in the least lost on her.

"I have to get back to Philly," Peter whispered, ever conscious that the timing of his travel plans was, once again, at the most inopportune time.

"We are having people to the house following the service. At what point are you planning on making your escape?" Hannah let the harsh words bite, knowing full well that he was trapped in her grip and could do little but stand there and take it. What did it matter, anyway? Her father—whom she loved with all her heart and with full belief that he loved her too, unconditionally—was gone.

Olivia began to squirm, and Marc, the second eldest, reached for her little hand and led her off to the car. Hannah wanted to descend into the open grave with Robert, to feel the comfort and protection that he always provided, even in the most tragic or unbearable of times. He was her rock. He was her mother's rock. And now, there he lay, cold and lifeless before everyone. Hannah longed to be ten years old again. To crawl into his lap and to wrap her arms around his massive neck and bury her head in his flannel shirt. He had felt like a giant when he lifted her up to carry her to bed, and would laugh when her pigtails brushed his cheek when he ducked to avoid bumping his head on the doorway into her ballerina pink bedroom with the white brass headboard and tulle cascading comforter on her bed. That was the daddy she remembered, that she had hoped to give her children in marrying a man like Peter. She had been wrong, so wrong.

And at that moment, she let self-pity consume her, because the truth was too much to bear. She would need to pull herself together and put on a face for the world— the one that they wanted to see. Not the broken and frightened version of the woman who should have all the answers. *Not today*, she had told herself. *Not today*.

She watched as they lowered the gleaming casket into

the ground. She comforted herself with the belief that somewhere, Robert's spirit was hovering above them at that very moment and would soon take its place in heaven, alongside his and Charlotte's beloved baby girl, who would finally get to feel the embrace of her magnificent father; where they would wait for Charlotte's beautiful soul to join them. Hannah needed to believe this more than anything.

CHAPTER 35

★ ★ ★

"YOU NEED TO EAT SOMETHING," Marney said, thrusting a plate in front of Hannah that contained a dollop of tuna salad, two deviled eggs, and a pickle.

When she shook her head, Marney placed it on the granite counter and then grabbed Hannah's shoulders, looking her squarely in the eyes. "You will get through this, I promise. You are Dr. Hannah. That doesn't mean you don't get to *feel* things. It's perfectly understandable."

Hannah let a tear slip down her cheek. She had thought that there simply weren't any more tears left in her. Yet, she could not turn them off.

Peter had left in a cab moments earlier, and she had watched from the kitchen window as Olivia played in the grass with her cousins.

The house was filled wall-to-wall with family and loved ones. Her sister, Muriel, had flown in with her husband, Dale, and would be staying on for the week before returning to Croatia and Muriel's work with the fellowship program with the National Science Foundation. Robert Jr.'s RV was parked indelicately on their front lawn, with the German Shepherds tethered to the back hitch gnawing on their plastic chew toys. His girlfriend, Chloe—a millennial with a myriad of tattoos and piercings that made her look like a New Mexico road map—was eyeing Hannah's broadcasting awards on the mantle. Hannah just wanted it all to be over so that she could retreat to her bed and escape the somber glances and the awkward condolences that affirmed, "At least your dear mother does not have to suffer knowing that he is gone," and "He loved you and your family so much. He was a great man." Hannah knew all of this, and yet the words bounced off of her ears and seemed to fall to the floor when spoken. She was grieving in a deep place inside of her that words and gestures simply could not reach. She'd wondered if that was how some of her callers and patients had felt—and the experience was making an impression upon her that only added to her desire to empathize more fully with others going through the grieving process. She knew all too well that it would be a process; only, she had little time to wait for the slow string of emotions that would ultimately lead to acceptance. She simply didn't have the time. She had a family to take care of, callers, patients, and a sick mother who needed her.

She dabbed her lashes with a wadded tissue and took a deep, cleansing breath. "No—I am okay, Marney. Really. I just need to take a beat here. I will be back full-force soon. I promise."

"No one is asking you to do anything you are not ready to do. Why don't you consider taking some time before jumping into the new gig? Spend some time with your family."

"My work is my salvation, Marney. I can do this. I *need* to keep doing what I do. The sooner, the better."

Marney nodded, hoping that Hannah was right. "Well, you are not alone. You have me." She squeezed Hannah's hand and handed her a beautiful vintage handkerchief with the letter "M" embroidered in the center. "Here, hang on to this."

At a time when everything in her fast-moving life felt so uncertain, it was nice to have a lifeline of her own. Hannah smiled.

>

CHAPTER 36

IT TOOK NO TIME AT all for Jon Novotny to quickly become Hannah's right *and* left arm. She needed the support and was grateful for his expertise. They thought the same thoughts, worked flawlessly in a cyclone of controlled chaos, finished each other's sentences, and had similar ideas for the show. They were linked in a symbiotic motion from prep to show-start, to sign-off.

Simply put, they were pure magic together. Jon was Hannah's champion, and she was his reason for believing in radio—*good* radio—once again.

"You want me to do what?" Hannah would ask, when Jon pitched a remote broadcast idea from a haunted hotel in the city or a surprise visit to a cheating boyfriend at his office or gym in order to confront him with a leaving spouse or lover's grievances. "We're not a reality show!" Hannah would quip and shoot him down. "What kind of credibility would *that* bring?"

"Credibility be damned!" Jon would retort. "We're out for ratings here."

Most typically, Hannah would compromise on less spectacular events that she felt were more aligned with her persona and expertise. She was happy to visit hospitals, women's shelters, and even a prison in order to bring her compassion and unique brand of psychological healing to the masses.

When she didn't have Hannah climbing into a dunk tank, or judging a chili cook-off at a local fair, Marney was keeping Hannah's calendar filled with paid personal appearances and endorsements to further her visibility and strengthen her brand.

Jon was a whiz, booking guests to appear on Hannah's show from various industries and social interests. This enabled her to hone her skills at live interviewing as she engaged with not only with callers and patients, but with renowned physicians, authors, and celebrities clamoring to get a chance to jump in the hot seat with her on her Friday afternoon broadcasts, where they would free-style and kibitz about any number of topics of the day. This made Hannah's show even more engaging and controversial—an outcome that Jon delighted in with aplomb.

When it came to ad buys, the station was nearly unable to handle the demand. Hannah's show was the top coveted time slot, with sponsors who much preferred Hannah's direct endorsement of their product or service to a pricey-produced jingle or thirty-second voice-over. Jon was genius at working product endorsements right into the fabric of the show, where Hannah would expound on the fantastic meal she had at a local restaurant or extol on the merits of any number of exceptional vitamin supplements or beauty products.

One day, Jon came to Hannah with a stunning suggestion. "I want to put your daughter, Olivia, on the mic for a spot for the local Kinder-Care ad. It will be a slam dunk!"

"Seriously?" Hannah hedged. "You are going to trust a six-year-old with a hot mic? Are you crazy? I mean, she's cute and smart and funny, but—"

"Exactly!" Jon clapped his hands and headed for Allison's office. "The boss lady is going to love this idea! Bring

Olivia in tomorrow and we'll lay down some recordings."

Hannah was skeptical, but she trusted Jon and knew that he would not make a fool of either her or Olivia, so she complied. *What could it hurt?* she'd reasoned. Kinder-Care was a huge local sponsor with national reach.

The next afternoon, Hannah appeared at the office with Olivia in tow, ready for her broadcasting debut. Little cherub-faced Olivia was wearing an adorable eyelet blue dress with a satin ribbon that matched Hannah's designer power suit, and she was carrying her favorite princess doll, Bella.

Jon set up a high stool in control room three, atop which he stacked two circular cushions. Hannah assisted him with placing the headphones astride Olivia's center braid, which caused her to giggle. The foam cover on the microphone was of particular fascination for her.

"Now, don't touch anything, sweetie," Hannah said from the stool beside her. Jon switched on the control panel, and soon she could hear him talking in her ear. She turned to Hannah and tittered.

"Can you hear Jon?" Hannah asked.

The little girl nodded.

"Here's what I want you to say," Jon instructed slowly. "I love Kinder-Care almost as much as listening to my mommy's show."

Olivia furled her ginger-tinged brows and took a huge breath. She spoke slowly and clearly into the microphone. "I wuv Kinda-Care, uh, almost I like listening to Mommy's show!"

"It's a take!" Jon shouted, ripping off his headphones. "This girl is a natural!"

Hannah laughed, shaking her head. "Are you sure? I mean, she can do it again. Maybe better."

"I'm good," Jon said, already cuing up the playback. "It was perfectly, *imperfect*. This will knock their socks off. Well, since she's here, maybe we'll do a couple more runs."

Hannah smiled. "What do you think, honey? Want to

try again?"

Olivia nodded and sat up straighter.

Why would Hannah even doubt her little angel? She was the best assistant she could ask for.

In sixteen months' time, *The Dr. Hannah Show* was heard on over one hundred fifty stations nationwide, and growing. It was the number-one rated format in talk radio, putting Hannah squarely in first place for the time slot. The tough-love tactics and resounding moral voice was being heard throughout the country loud and clear. It was not bunk or pop-philosophy. It was true wisdom—at fifty thousand watts.

Hannah would continue to hold the hearts and fascination of listeners for the next nine years; reaching, at its peak, four hundred stations nationally with over ten million listeners, with designs to move her exclusively to the no-holds-barred medium of satellite broadcasting at the renewal of her contract in 2015. Such was the spell Hannah had cast on audiences, who were glued to their radios each day from eleven until two o'clock. Now, not just the nation, but the *world* was listening.

CHAPTER 37

★ ★ ★

HARRISBURG, PA
SEPTEMBER 11, 2011

THE BOY SAT RIVETED TO his seat, staring at the television screen at the front of the classroom that the teacher, Ms. Stevenson, had switched on in commemoration of the event. Together, the entire sixth-grade class watched in silence as the image of a New York skyscraper loomed ablaze, frightfully incinerating the souls inside. The footage was over a decade old, yet the news bulletin seemed as if it were occurring in real-time, an inescapable drama unfolding on the screen. It was not the first time the boy and his classmates had seen the footage from the ill-famed day that took place when he and his peers were just one year old. It had become a piece of history that had been woven into their minds and psyches throughout their young lives, never losing its power to induce shock and horror in the hearts and minds of Americans, who remembered the unthinkable scene that had befallen the World Trade Center on September 11th, 2001. The stoic teacher silenced a few nervous snickers coming from the back row with a sharp *"Shhhh!"* and directed the students to watch as a befuddled redhead from a national news station reported the account. The entire class gave a collective gasp and cringed as they watched as the second aircraft appeared on the screen, piercing the skin of tower number two; its twin withering beneath black clouds of death smoke roiling into the blue sky.

The boy watched with rapt fascination as bodies emerged from the broken glass windows like lifeless paper dolls that seemed to float in slow motion through the air. He had the face of an angel, innocent and pure. Fair-skinned and freckled. It was the kind of face that could sell breakfast cereal or mac and cheese ads. He wet his lips and leaned forward to take in the macabre images flickering on the screen, just as he had done many times before. This was his favorite part.

Ms. Stevenson made the sign of the cross, remembering the exact day when she had been teaching a similar class of students that fated morning, when they had all been informed via the school intercom of the chilling terror unfolding. She had calmly asked the class she was entrusted with that day, which had begun to erupt with chatter and confusion, to join in a collective prayer. And they did. Every last one had bowed their heads; some of the girls were clinging to one another and were crying.

When the documentary ended, the staid teacher let the credits roll and kept the lights off for a moment of reverent silence. "Let's bow our heads now, if you wish to, in remembrance," she said. Everyone present in the rows of thirty-one metal desks paused and prayed with her—everyone except for the boy. He was still staring at the screen, strangely transfixed, and then he scrawled something in red ink across his notebook—something that caused him to smile.

CHAPTER 38

★ ★ ★

VENTURE MEDIA RADIO STATION
JUNE 15. 2015

THE DECISION TO END HER marriage was gut-wrenching. A simple letter, the first of several more to come, in Peter's handwriting, had been placed on her bureau on the day that he left her. Two hand-written pages traded for thirty-eight years of marriage and a hundred thousand lies between them. He had written her from Philadelphia, where he had intended on staying until the end. His lover, Anthony, a young man she had never met, yet who knew the intimate details of her and Peter's lives, was dying of AIDS in a hospice, where Peter was now keeping vigil, day and night.

They had, shockingly, been lovers for over ten years, the letter had said, starting with: *My dear Hannah, it pains me so to write this, but I must be truthful if I am worth anything at all. God knows, you deserve to know the truth* . . . .

Hannah shuddered. *Ten years!* Peter had confessed everything in vivid detail. He sent additional letters to Hannah in the weeks that followed in an effort to explain his tormented thoughts and tortured heart, not to beg forgiveness, nor ask to come home. Perhaps, she later thought, in an attempt to relieve himself of the guilt. To help him understand it all himself. But still, she could not believe this was happening.

She received the first letter just four months ago, days after their anniversary. It went on: *Maybe it was never "true love" that I had with you—you who had all the answers all the time; so far on the right that everything seemed so simple when you took out the emotion; the human need. Well, my dear, you certainly found a way to make that illusion pay off for you. And because of this, I know that you and our children will be all right. Take the new job. I know you will shine. You deserve it—you have earned it. They will love you. After this is over, I'm going to go away. I'm not sure where, but it will take a good long time for me to rebuild my life and heal my soul. I have submitted my resignation at the hospital. I don't think that I will be looking to practice medicine again. Not for a while.*

I have shared these details with no one except you, because of the highly personal nature. I trust you will be discreet, as you have always proven to be, although you certainly owe me nothing in light of all that has happened.

Hannah folded the letter for the hundredth time, placing it carefully back in her purse beneath her desk. Nobody else knew this ugly little secret, except for Marney, of course. They had worked hard to make sure of that. They would wait, as agreed for everyone's benefit, to tell the world about the divorce until after her birthday party and the announcement of her syndicated contract renewal and the news of her garnering *the* position of her career—still in the finalizing stages that she would not yet let herself believe was real.

And the children? What would she say to them? *"Hold on to your hats, kids—your father's a homosexual."* The thought of it was simply unbearable.

Peter's words were more than just another sad and lonely

cry as from a host of misguided souls in a sea of countless emails, letters, and texts that poured across her desk
daily. And to herself, his shattered wife who received them,
she had to ask: What words of wisdom would she have
to offer? To whom would Dr. Hannah turn for answers?
She wondered, as she stared at the blinking cursor on the
screen: *Why now? Why did Peter choose to unburden himself
with the truth at this time? After so many years?* When things
were going so well and their futures were about to take
even greater flight? It was bittersweet, to say the least. It
only left her more confused. These were questions that not
even the astute Dr. Hannah could answer.

She stared at the screen, and then at the contract for
Global Network looming on her desk. Never had she had
such an opportunity to shine. Never before had her plate
been quite so full, and yet, she felt so positively empty
inside. She felt like a fraud. At age sixty, she was about
to face life as a divorcee. Hadn't she had enough of the
callers' and listeners' sob stories and incessant ranting? She
was tired. Damn weary of it all. Yet, the only way she knew
how to heal her own soul was to move ahead. To challenge
herself once again—to do and be *more*.

The biggest realization being, that with this new reality,
and all the uncertainty that lay ahead, she was uncharacteristically afraid. She clicked on the button, her gaze
transfixed on the screen, ironically sending the comic—
and her future—into the stratosphere.

CHAPTER 39
★ ★ ★

(TWO MONTHS EARLIER – APRIL 2015)

"WHO PEED IN YOUR CORNFLAKES?" Marney said, powering down her phone to avoid interruptions. Why on earth Hannah insisted on meeting in a church pew at St. Joseph Roman Catholic Church baffled her. Further, she would have to watch the potty mouth in the hallowed chamber of the early 19th-century landmark.

She'd flown in at Hannah's request. Marney had not ever heard Hannah sound so unhinged as when she spoke to her on the phone that morning, and frankly, it had spooked her. "What's going on?" she'd asked, responding to Hannah's sixth text message that morning with a call. "Are you having second thoughts about re-signing with Venture Media? Because if you are—"

"No, it's not about that. I am just struggling with something, and I wanted to talk it out. I guess, I'm saying that I need your advice," Hannah had said. "Can you come here?"

Within an hour, Marney was booked on the next flight out to Akron-Canton Regional Airport. She jumped in a rental car and headed to the address that Hannah had proffered. When she pulled up to the ancient brownstone building at Sackett and Second Streets with its stained glass windows and manicured gardens, she shuddered. *What balagan was this?* she'd wondered. That Hannah wanted to talk to her in a church, of all places?

"Thanks for coming. I really am at a loss here, and I need to figure out what I need to do," Hannah said in a voice just above a whisper. She was kneeling, and had obviously been praying. Marney was secretly hoping that she would not burst into flames and *pizootz* right there for setting even a stiletto on the grounds of such a sanctuary—not that she was a stellar Jewess by any means. Her relationship with the Almighty was relegated to a vague observance of the high holidays and cries for mercy when suffering a particularly miserable hangover. For the most part, she was a wretched example of piety.

"I have a deep affection for this place," Hannah said, sliding her rump onto the hard, weathered bench. "I went to grade school here when my family moved to Ohio. I started in the sixth grade with a nun for my teacher named Sr. Felicity."

Marney sat next to her and settled in, letting Hannah get to where she was going.

"All of our kids attended St. Joseph's too. Even Olivia—she had a lay teacher, though, for most of her elementary classes. Times change so quickly."

Marney did not know about such things as nuns and May Crownings, and Sunday mass. Still, she could imagine Olivia all dolled up in white lace with her rosary and little prayer book when she was young, a far cry from the somber, soft-spoken young girl with the soulful, quiet stare who kept to writing in her journal most of the time, trying to go unnoticed in the halls of her high school and social circles to avoid being teased for being the daughter of the outspoken "Dr. Hannah." No one said it would be easy to blend in; *that*, Marney did know a thing or two about.

"The original church was started in 1883 as a mission. Then the new church was dedicated on June 19th way back in 1887. That's why I've always loved it; I've felt *connected* to it somehow because we share the same birthday, this church and I." Hannah smiled, and then wiped a tear that had escaped from her languid blue eye.

Marney took her hand.

Hannah shuddered and then said, "Peter is not coming back to us. Not ever. There is

someone . . . else." Hannah let the words do their worst to both relieve and ravish her with the power of it now being spoken out loud. In God's house, no less.

"What? An affair?" Marney said in a fervent whisper.

Hannah sniffled. "Worse than that—he's apparently *gay*." She breathed the words and let them fall in the emptiness of the massive space, along with a stream of hot tears.

"*What?*" Marney blurted, sanctity be damned. "You have got to be shitting me!"

An old woman wearing a kerchief looked up from her bent prayer book five pews away and shot them an appalled look before shuffling out toward the confessionals.

Hannah riffled through her handbag for tissue and began dabbing at her eyes apologetically. "I am sorry. I don't usually break down like this. It's just that it is all so raw. Even though I suspected something was different—for a very long time—I could *never* have imagined this."

Marney took a cleansing breath and squeezed Hannah's hand tighter.

"There's more," Hannah said, dabbing at the smudges of mascara that were bleeding from her blonde lashes.

"*More?*" Marney was in need of air. She wondered if the holy water was for anybody.

"His . . . lover, of five years is dying. He has AIDS," Hannah said, now looking Marney directly in the eyes.

"And Peter. Does he—?" Marney asked, her heart at a

standstill.

"No, thank God," Hannah said, then, looking upward at the crucifix, she closed her eyes tightly.

"He's clean."

Marney slumped with relief and drew in a full breath. "*Barux hashem!* Thank God."

The two sat in silence for what seemed like an eternity. Finally, Marney turned to Hannah and said, "Let's get out of here. You look like we both could use a drink."

CHAPTER 40
★ ★ ★

MARNEY FOLLOWED HANNAH'S SHINY SUV to a Hilton in Fairlawn with a bar and grill with views of a sprawling pond. They sat at a table overlooking the water as the sun was beginning to set.

"I can't drink. I'm on the air in a few hours," Hannah said.

"Fine. I'll drink for both of us," Marney said, ordering a stiff concoction from the bar menu.

"Light on the adornments and heavy on the rum," she said, waving off the waiter. "It's five o'clock somewhere."

Hannah sighed. "What am I going to do?"

"You are going to move upward and onward, that's what," Marney had said, digging into her giant designer purse the size of a football stadium and pulling out a stack of documents fastened with a metal clip that had become a bit dog-eared from the journey, but was overall, no worse for wear. It was the renewal contract for Venture Media prepared to offer Hannah four more years of exclusive syndication and a premiere satellite broadcast channel of her own—*The Dr. Hannah Channel*. Marney once again had poured her heart and soul into the negotiations. It was a fine and lucrative deal, and in her mind, only the beginning. The document was amply covered with yellow sticky tabs, indicating where she should initial and sign. Marney plopped it onto the white tablecloth. "I reviewed it thoroughly. It's tight. All it needs is for you to give it your John Hancock."

Hannah stared at the offering. It had been everything she had worked for—everything that she'd wanted. The moment had finally arrived, yet somehow, she couldn't bring herself to feel happy. Not yet, anyway.

"Well? The best way to handle all this is to get back in there and claim what you have earned. You owe it to yourself—to your family—and to your listeners." Marney handed her the Goliath contract and smiled.

Hannah knew that Marney was right. She *had* earned it. She would move forward whatever that meant, and regret nothing. She would have to.

They ate a late lunch and discussed plans for the radio show moving forward. Hannah half-listened as Marney droned on. She had a never-say-die attitude. Hannah felt lucky to have her in her corner. Hannah had her leftovers packed in a Styrofoam box for her dinner later, when she would warm it up in the microwave sometime before Olivia would waltz into the house after dark, saying that she had eaten at her friend Skyler's, then slink off to her room, brooding. She was taking her parents' separation very hard. On so many levels, Hannah felt that she had failed all of the family, but none as much as Olivia. Hannah sighed fretfully. "How am I going to tell them about their dad?"

"You, my friend, will figure it out. You are Dr. Hannah to the world, but to your kids—you are the greatest mom on Earth," Marney said, reapplying her vixen red lipstick in a vintage compact mirror.

"I think that Ty and Marc will understand, but Broderick and Olivia will struggle with it, each in their own way, I'm certain. I have to be ready for that, and do all that I can to help them cope with whatever feelings they will have as a result," Hannah said, staring into her coffee cup.

"Wait and see, Hannah," Marney said, blowing on her espresso. "There is so much more ahead for you. I just know it. And I am going to help you get it. Remember, living well is the best revenge."

Hannah nodded. But it was not revenge that she wanted. Nothing about the future seemed well-timed or comfortable.

"What about a break?" Marney said. "I had a blast a few weeks ago taking that extended spa weekend by myself in Maui, and it was heavenly. Did some damage on my Amex, but it was way worth it!"

That explained the deep tan across Marney's laugh lines, Hannah thought.

"Why don't you have your assistant at the station book you a getaway somewhere on a beach? You can tape a few shows in advance, or run a 'best-of' marathon. Let that producer-guru, Jon, take care of things while you're gone. It would do you a world of good."

Hannah smiled. "I can't get away that easily, Marney—I have too many obligations here. The station will never go for that, plus I have patients at the clinic. I will just dive into my work, and that will have to do."

"Well, you should be the one calling the shots," Marney said. "It's *your* show. Hey—I've got it. Let's leverage things. We need to celebrate this re-signing—and your sixtieth birthday is coming up in June, right, like you mentioned in the church."

"Don't remind me" Hannah moaned.

"Why, then, don't we plan a party where we officially announce your contract renewal *and* celebrate you turning sixty? I can hold off with the press for a while on the news of the re-signing. We'll make it a publicity event and do a big reveal with a giant cake, all that kind of crap. People will eat it up."

Hannah paused and thought about the suggestion. *A new decade and a new start. Why not?* "Okay," she said, sliding up from her chair. "I'm on board for that, but nothing about my personal business to the press. It has to appear that everything is the way it was. No one needs to know a thing about the divorce. We will keep it on the down-low for a while longer."

"Agreed," Marney said, smiling. *Did Hannah really just say, 'down-low'?* "Of course, I'll not say a word."

Marney could do more than bite her tongue, but the truth was, it was killing her to keep the biggest secret of all, under her hat—that she had also been working on a deal of the century that would change Hannah's, and her life, exceedingly. No deals were off limits, and Hannah was basically a free agent, as she did not have a non-compete clause with Venture. She could, in essence, write her own ticket. Marney would wait to be sure. No sense in tempting the fates. Marney's "spa getaway weekend" may have turned out to be the business opportunity of a lifetime, with the potential to be more blazing than a volcanic hot stone massage. If it all played out right, she was certain that Hannah's ship was about to come in. All she could do was put her faith in the future and watch the horizon.

CHAPTER 41
★ ★ ★

JUST THREE WEEKS EARLIER, MARNEY remarkably found herself sitting across from none other than network producer Bumpy Friedman from Global Networks, who held the key to Hannah's, and her, fate. The meeting was a result of a chance encounter three days prior at the ritzy resort where she was staying in Maui. She had inadvertently run into network executive Stone Kendall, in, of all places, the elevator at the Grand Wailea—a predicament that did little to hurt her cause of advancing her client to the top of the short list of hopefuls for Global Network's newest daytime talk show pilot. When she overheard Kendall discussing the show pilot with his associate on a slow ride down to the fragrant lobby, she could not believe her luck. Not being one to miss an opportunity, Marney hit the *Stop* button on the control panel, buying twenty precious suspended minutes to literally give the best elevator sales pitch ever over the sound of the tinny alarm.

"I think that your network will be most interested in my client. Have you seen Dr. Hannah's numbers?" Marney had said, sealing the deal with the presentation of her splashy business card and an invitation for the show producers to visit Hannah's New York studio to see her in action.

Stone was not surprised. It happened more than one would think. But later, when he called Bumpy to relay that he was just handed radio psychologist juggernaut, Dr. Hannah Courtland-Murphy's name for consideration, he was met with a heavy dose of elation.

"Are you for *real*, man?" Bumpy howled from across the Pacific. "She was the inspiration for this whole gab-fest concept in the first place." He had remembered dialing into the radio shrink's show in his pickup on the way back to the studio from the grocery store the fated day that destiny came to save his ass and the idea for *The Gab*, was born. He was already a fan, having heard a live clip of Hannah in action before ever receiving Stone Kendall's call seemingly on-cue. He couldn't believe his dumb luck.

"I'm telling you, man"—Kendall chuckled—"if Dr. Hannah is as convincing as her take-no-prisoners-ballsy agent, then I'd say, you've got a winner there."

Bumpy knew that Hannah had the sense of authority and credibility that would work effectively to balance out an all-women host panel. Plus, she was smart, attractive, and relatable—a triple threat. Bumpy was certain that the nation's love affair with the sassy radio shrink would transfer to television, and unabashedly agreed to give Marney a meeting.

Kendall shook his head. It was like old times. "She'd be a ringer, for sure. It would set the tone for the rest of the cast," he said into his phone. "What do you say, Boss?"

Bumpy popped the tab on a warm Diet Coke to celebrate. "Get Hannah's agent in here, pronto—and we'll talk turkey. Then, let's find the next one!"

From the island, Marney had already arranged to have a courier hand-deliver several promotional packets, a stack of audiotapes, and ratings reports personally to the gleaming

New York office. She followed suit with a phone call and several texts to secure a meeting with the eccentric Bumpy Friedman. Marney had decided that she would only tell Hannah if there was a real chance of her being considered for one of the four co-anchor positions—in addition to her current radio renewal offer—to persuade her to take on yet another career move adding to her already-full plate. She would keep Hannah so booked and busy with her fast-growing celebrity and brand that she would long forget her own broken heart, and that Peter Murphy had ever been deserving of sharing her revered limelight.

CHAPTER 42

★ ★ ★

MAY 4. 2015

IT WAS NOT A HARD sell after all. Show producer Bumpy Friedman was more than happy to meet their terms, and would soon have himself a bona fide pop psychologist on his all-women host panel. When Marney received the call saying that Hannah officially got the job, she could hardly contain herself. She caught the last evening flight to Ohio and was waiting for Hannah at the radio station with a bottle of champagne to deliver the news after her show.

"What are we celebrating?" Hannah said, settling into her swivel chair and kicking her heels off in exchange for her more sensible office flats.

"You!" Marney smiled, producing two Solo cups, which was the best she could pillage from the staff kitchen. "How do you feel about daytime talk shows?"

"I have one!" Hannah said, pointing to her desk and very complicated piles of medical journals, awards, and binders of cume ratings and share reports.

"No, I mean—*television* talk shows," Marney said, waiting a beat.

"Well, I suppose they are fine, but most of them are very boring."

"Exactly! And why do you suppose?" Marney hedged.

"No substance. I mean, sizzle is fine, but you have to have real discussions, right?" Hannah said and then watched as Marney's smile broke wide. Then she gasped. "You *didn't!*"

"I did. I put your name in the hat for Global Network's newest venture—an all-women talk show that will be airing in the fall—and you got the gig. You are going to be the resident mental well-being expert!" Marney squealed as she held out a copy of the contract before Hannah's disbelieving eyes. "If you want to, of course," Marney said slyly as she placed the offering into Hannah's hands gingerly.

Hannah blanched when she saw the terms. It was more money than she could have ever imagined her radio show garnering in a *five*-year run.

"It ain't chump change," Marney said, holding up the bottle of bubbly and waiting another beat. "I met with Global Network, and they are amicable with you continuing on with your syndicated radio show and plans for further satellite distribution *along* with doing the tapings of the talk show. We will rework the contracts. No reason you can't do it all."

Hannah took a deep breath. Everything was about to change anyway, and the one thing she could fully embrace was doing more good for others. Anything to keep her going and to build her brand of championing empowerment for women. It would put her squarely on the road to a fresh start. "Yes!" Hannah said, surprising herself. "Tell them I will do it." Hannah then laughed, cried, and then laughed some more. She was mostly in shock. "I can't believe it," she said, settling into her swivel chair. *Was the room actually spinning?* "I take it this is the work of your brilliant negotiation skills?"

Marney wiped a tear that had already slipped from her cat-lined eye. "It *is* what I do. Really, Hannah, this is such a sweet deal. What can I say? They *wanted* you. Apparently, you were part of the producer's vision from the start."

Hannah took a deep breath and then reached to embrace Marney with trembling arms. "Thank you," she said, and then pulled a serious frown. "Do you think we should have asked for more?"

The two women broke into laughter and then hugged some more.

"You know, you're going to have to put those heels back on. Television is a visual medium!" Marney said, popping the cork and pouring out two generous cups full of the pricey champagne and handing one out to Hannah. "Here's to that bright future of yours, Hannah. Here's to you! You are going to be one busy bitch!" She howled.

Hannah took a sip and smiled. *What had she done?*

Marney rattled on, "They are looking to do the official signing as a group once they have the other cast members chosen. It will be at the end of August, with the pilot kicking off in the fall. Now we will have another wonderful announcement to reveal at your sweet-sixty party!" Marney proclaimed, raising up the red cup. "Dr. Hannah Courtland-Murphy—one of the newest divas of daytime talk!"

Hannah's heart pounded. There would be no backing out once she signed.

Marney was an unstoppable train. "Not a word about this to anyone, okay? Let me work out all the details with the rest of the promotional team." She grinned. There was an offer from Ricon Broadcasting out of Toronto currently pending that would work nicely as a ruse. Marney would continue to let them think they had a shot. It would block the news from leaking and keep the press at bay. "Didn't I tell you that you were going to explode, Hannah? This is it—*this* gig with Global Network is the opportunity of a lifetime, and it is going to boost your career to even greater heights." Marney then planted a lipstick imprint onto Hannah's cheek. "It's your time, sweetie."

Hannah felt as dizzy as the bubbles dancing in the cup. What did she know about television? Marney was going to have to be certain enough for both of them.

CHAPTER 43
★ ★ ★

AUGUST 13, 2015

T HE BOY WITH THE RUDDY cheeks had grown into a sullen, insidious teen who thought himself to be invincible. He had them all fooled. Every last one of them. From rudimentary and polite appearances at family gatherings to acing the Dean's List, he was a tenth-grader who had perfected the art of pleasing adults and blending in.

He was a quiet genius with eccentric interests: World War II movies, sci-fi graphic novels, physics brainteasers, and computer gaming. He was a whiz with anything electronic. He was especially adept at computer programming. He thought nothing of applying his brilliant talents to the task of manipulating and hacking files, just for fun.

He started off with the small stuff, in junior high, innocent "pranks," in which he crafted clever ploys for besieging unknown hosts with innocently cloaked computer viruses that arrived innocuously on various hard drives in email boxes throughout the country under various aliases that, when opened, ultimately kicked out damaging directives that wiped out entire days, weeks, months of data. Or, in some cases, shutting down the host's computer completely, causing permanent and irrefutable damage to the users' hard drive.

When Sun Printing suffered an all-company network shutdown for five straight days last October due to a terminal computer virus, it drove the company into full-scale crisis. When the company president appeared four weeks later on the evening news, declaring financial ruin, and stating that the business was being forced to close its doors after twenty-three years, it was he who took the bow from his secret den of destruction—a teenager's bedroom somewhere in obscurity. A room that was strewn throughout with unopened text books, black-lit concert posters, sweat socks, and propagandist magazines hid discreetly under a bed with faded *Star Wars* sheets, along with enough ammunition and explosives concealed in duffel bags and backpacks to blow away an entire city block and the people he hated.

Which was exactly what he intended to do.

CHAPTER 44

★ ★ ★

MAY 2015

HANNAH HAD AGREED TO MEET with Peter when he had said that he wanted to discuss a few things, namely, their daughter, Olivia. Hannah knew that she need not worry about him changing the conditions of the language in the divorce settlement because it was ironclad. Olivia would remain in Hannah's custody, as per the agreement awarding Peter specified visitation time of every other weekend during the school year, various holidays, and two full weeks over summer break.

Peter's relationship with his daughter was solid. In fact, he often spent time with her to make up for the fact that he and Hannah worked such demanding schedules that often left Olivia either shuffled from sitters and nannies, or dragged along to client meetings and sessions. Her siblings were much older, and particularly when Broderick left the house to start school in Arizona, Olivia was relegated to being an only child, so to speak. By the time she was in middle school, she was basically a latchkey kid, who became quite proficient at taking care of herself. To make up for a myriad of guilt-laden decisions on both of their parts, Hannah and Peter tried to indulge their daughter any way they could. It was nothing for Peter to show up with tickets for a ski-weekend in Aspen for some father-daughter bonding time, knowing full well that Hannah could not join them due to the restrictions of her show schedule. This, she'd felt, Peter used to his advantage, as he was quickly becoming the "nice" or "buddy" parent, which infuriated Hannah. Wasn't it she who would often rightfully counsel her listeners and patients to avoid this "over giving" of material possessions in exchange for a child's love? Still, it was Peter who reveled in treating Olivia to a trip to Vancouver for the Winter Olympics when she was ten; and later, to a Taylor Swift concert on her thirteenth birthday in Denver, complete with backstage passes at the Pepsi Center. He bought her every electronic device—somehow managing to be first in line at the Apple store to the get the newest gadget, which he would have promptly downloaded with all of her favorite music. Hannah simply could not compete with his fly-in-and-fly-out schedule that would have him whisking Olivia away to a different city every other weekend, or on some fun adventure that decidedly left her behind, albeit the trips had steadily begun to diminish as of late. Either way, Hannah secretly resented him for it.

What in the world could he want to talk about? Hannah had wondered on the drive into the city to meet with Peter at a bristling pub in the Arts District. He had been virtually silent since leaving the letter three months earlier, like a coward, just days after their thirty-eighth anniversary—the letter telling her that his heart had no love for her, that he loved a man, and that he couldn't stay. Since then, the communication had been limited to the pricey quarter-hour calls and emails and texts from the lawyers. Cold, impersonal language about the sorting out of a lifetime together regarding real estate, china place settings, bank holdings, and scheduled visits with the minor child, Olivia Murphy.

It was all she could do to keep it together a while longer, before the news of their divorce would be made public and she would then have the shame and pity of all of America—right on the heels of her syndicate contract renewal and debut television appearance on *The Gab*. She would fight to hold her head high and serve as a beacon for all women everywhere who have had to carry the unspeakable burden of divorce. She would know how they felt. How they carried their pain throughout their daily lives, as they would go about the business of being good mothers, citizens, and friends. This would be her task and calling. It would be the platform by which she would help others like herself find their way back to themselves—to heal.

When she arrived, Peter was standing to greet her, looking frazzled and exhausted. His chestnut hair had grayed significantly in the past several months, or maybe she hadn't noticed until now. His eyes were solemn, and with the five-o'clock shadow covering his sallow skin, he looked for the first time in her recollection, disheveled.

"What's going on?" Hannah said coolly, and she took the seat across from him at a booth near the window. She was all business.

"Thank you for coming."

The waiter appeared and asked if she wanted a drink.

"Rosé," Peter said before she could answer. Then he checked himself. "That is, if that is what you want to drink," he said, gripping the bottle of imported beer, his once-steady surgeon's hands sweating nervously.

"Rosé is find, thank you," Hannah said, settling in.

The waiter left, and she leaned forward, to sit a bit taller. "So, you wanted to talk. Let's talk."

Peter gave a little sniff. She was ever the pushy show host. The caller only got fifteen seconds to lay out the request or problem at hand. Why should this be any different? He began, "I do want to talk to you about Olivia, but first you need to know how I got here—how *we* got here. That is, if you want to know."

Hannah's drink arrived, and she took a slow sip and thought better of burying her head or walking away. It would not be easy to hear, but she needed to know.

"Okay," she said. "I am listening."

CHAPTER 45
★ ★ ★

BRENTWOOD, TN

B EING PETER MURPHY WAS NEVER the stuff of heroes or handsome leading men-types that they make Lifetime movies about or showered with accolades for humanitarian contributions to the world and works of selfless love and peace. Instead, he had managed to stay just under the radar all his life, preferring instead, to blend into the background and keep his nose to the grindstone, even after discovering that he had a unique and sharp mind that few rivaled. By age sixteen he had already been "placed ahead" in school two levels at the prestigious college-preparatory academy that his parents worked tirelessly in the family business to provide their firstborn and only son every advantage in life. As long as Peter could remember, all he wanted to do was to be a cardiologist and fix what was broken. A heart attack had blindsided his paternal grandfather when Peter was six, and he had never forgotten the pledge he had made to himself to become a doctor. It was really the only goal he could recall ever having—and he intended to reach it. It was as simple as that.

Ingrid and Jamison Murphy were Peter's immigrant parents. They had emigrated to the U.S. when they were both young children. Ingrid's parents were from Warsaw and Jamison's from Dublin, both fleeing the perils of violence and oppression for the shores of America, where they found work in the Depression-ravished tobacco and cotton crops in North Carolina, where both of their families had settled. It was there that the two met as children. In order to make a living, families at that time needed to use all available children to work alongside them in the fields, so Ingrid and Jamison worked dutifully with their families in the hot sun. Some years later, Jamison's family started growing food crops with the help of the government. The women in their coterie then learned the skill of canning, which served to revitalize and further secure the immigrant families' livelihoods. This ultimately allowed Ingrid and Jamison to eventually be able to go to school and to trade the fieldwork for schoolbooks. They had known each other all of their lives, first working side by side in the improvised fields, and later learning arithmetic, and playing in the dirt piles made by relief workers laboring to rebuild the new roads into town. The two knew little about life in a New World, except for what they discovered together and were able to make for themselves. At eighteen, having fallen in love, they got married, and left the Carolina farm life for the lure of urban expansion, and headed westward to Nashville.

In 1945 Jamison sank all he had into a roadside business selling handcrafted woodwork items that he had made, keeping to the basics with sturdy-backed stools, chairs, and rocking cradles for infants that were crafted as beautiful as they were practical. Soon, the demand for his handiwork enabled the young couple to save enough money to purchase a small lean-to shack that served as a small storefront in which Jamison could sell his wares. The young couple slept on a cot in the back, while Ingrid cleaned the homes of Nashville's elite and came home to cook on a rickety coal stove that brought warmth and sustenance to their lives. Within seven years, they had been blessed with a mortgage on a small brick storefront with an attached apartment and the miracle of a little one of their own on the way, after fearing that they were infertile. Due to complications with the birth, however, Peter would be their one and only child. Still, he was their one special blessing. He was perfect in every way, and to his loving parents, the promise of more than just an American dream—he held the key to their very legacy, and upon his little shoulders, they heaped every expectation and hope that they could for his success and happiness.

By the time Peter was twelve, the family furniture business had grown in scale, and the Murphys had begun to make a name for themselves, attracting buyers from as far away as Chicago. Eventually, the Murphy name would come to grace over twenty-five store franchises in neighboring cities throughout the South as well as across the state.

Growing up with the incessant expectations of his immigrant parents, Peter knew that his success in life meant more than anything—to them. He rarely allowed himself the normal comforts and distractions of childhood that his friends were enjoying. In 1966, when boys his age were becoming acquainted with the TV series *Batman*, watching as "Mean" Joe Greene dominated college football at the University of Texas, and ogling American sex symbol Raquel Welch on the big screen, Peter was marveling at groundbreaking news on the medical front of surgeon Dr. Michael De Bakey, who implanted an artificial heart into the chest of a coal miner. Peter Murphy was, it seemed, anything but an average kid.

Peter's freshman year of high school brought to light further talents that Ingrid and Jamison reveled in bragging about. It seemed that Peter was quite the natural swimmer. He had speed, power, and a freestyle stroke that broke records at every junior varsity swim meet he participated in. Surprisingly, he enjoyed the sport and found the competition to be a natural rush. Quickly, early-morning and mid-day workouts became his daily routine, further isolating him from his peers and placing him on-par with the upperclassmen elite and varsity coaches who were the only ones pounding drills at six a.m.

He loved the feel of the water streaming along his body and the way that the training had strengthened his biceps, back, and pectoral muscles. By age seventeen, he had developed into a chiseled, lean athlete, having grown three inches, cinching winning lead after winning lead that left his competition trailing behind him. Everyone noticed the change in his demeanor and confidence. It was also remarkably fulfilling for him to challenge and push himself to greater heights. Finally, he had found something other than academics at which to excel. Even his parents backed his verve for the sport and lauded his many wins, proudly boasting and displaying his state medals on the walls of their flagship store.

One person, in particular, who had been instrumental in Peter's training and development was Tory Robinson, the school's swim coach. Tory was a whiz with the student athletes, and treated each one of them as if they were Olympians. It was his way to be friendly but firm with them in guiding them to big wins for the school. One of the things that drew students to Tory was the casual, relatable way that he talked to teens, never condescending like so many of the teachers and adults grappling with the weight of the world upon them, so it seemed. Tory was down-to-earth, and Peter liked that about him. Socially awkward in every other situation, Peter felt strangely secure and content when he swam. It was his solace and his salvation—those early-morning laps at the pool, just him and Tory's whistle drills, cheering him on.

Hannah had not ever remembered Peter mentioning having been a swimmer in his high school years. She had only ever known him to play Lacrosse in college—and quite well. "You've never mentioned this," Hannah said with as little judgment as she could manage, and fearing what was to come next.

Peter paused, and swallowed hard. "It didn't take him long to single me out and take advantage. That is what he did. He *took advantage* of me." His voice trailed off and Hannah painfully reached for Peter's hand across the table, letting him tell his truth.

"What happened?"

"He invited me over to his 'pad' he called it. I innocently agreed. We were going to watch some swimming tapes of my last meet. He said that he would slip me a beer. That it would be our secret." Peter's eye twitched like it did when he was feeling anxious, and his lip began to quiver. "I wanted him to think I was cool. You know, that I could be down with that."

"Instead?" Hannah coaxed.

"Instead, he came on to me not two seconds after I walked into his apartment and he shut the door. He reached for me. He touched me." Peter said the words plainly, just as a tear escaped from his right eye. He quickly caught it before it rolled all the way down his cheek to his chin. "I pushed him hard and threw him off of me. I called him a fucking faggot and bolted out of there. I ran all the way back to my car."

"What did you do then?" Hannah asked. "Where did you go?"

"I went home. I walked past my parents in the living room like nothing had happened, and I went up to my bedroom. I laid on the floor there next to my bed, then crawled into the bathroom, doubled over with pains stabbing me in the gut. I couldn't breathe. I thought I was going to die. And do you know why?"

Hannah shook her head pensively.

"Here's the thing. I *wanted* h im to do it. I did. Only I couldn't admit that to myself. I couldn't accept it. Not then. I lived a lie from that day forward. Every time the subject ever came up, I was the one with the homophobic retorts and flexing my muscles to the world, and years later, holding up my perfect wife and family for the entire world to see, while all the time, denying the truth. I would just end up on some bathroom floor somewhere and writhe in real physical pain. And worse than all of that was the fact that I couldn't admit it to myself, and I took you and the family on that ride with me."

Hannah glanced away. *Was this an apology?*

She had heard it all before. Countless times. Women callers lamenting that their "heterosexual" husbands were caught watching gay porn, or checking out another guy on the sly; texting someone incessantly but insisting that there was "no other woman." Who was the bigger fool? The one *playing the game,* or the one *being played?* She, for once, did not have the answer.

CHAPTER 46

★ ★ ★

MAY 2015

HANNAH HAD PLANNED THE LOVELIEST Saturday. First, she and Olivia would grab a stress-free hour yoga class at the hip new studio on Front Street with the teal and bamboo wood lounge area that served the most incredible vitamin-infused mineral water. Then, they would be off to the thrift store circuit and open air market, where they could try on floppy hats and peruse the local farm-to-table produce that Hannah used to make her famous vegetarian chili. It had already been a full year since Olivia had decided that she had sworn off eating meat, and it was a good bet that she was sticking to her convictions. This was no surprise to Hannah. Much like herself, when Olivia committed herself to something, she stuck to it.

They opted for two frozen yogurt cups and sat on a bench near a skate park. They watched as skinny young boys in ripped jeans zipped around the plaza on two wheels, jumping over hand railings along concrete steps and curbs onto large, curved ramps.

"Your brother could do all that," Hannah said, wincing.

"Not that I was happy about it."

"Broderick *used* to be able to do that," Olivia corrected. "Now he wouldn't risk messing up his perfect Danny Zuko hair with even a sun visor caddying for that golf pro in Scottsdale." Broderick still loved the game, and was paying his dues while currently getting his MBA out West.

"How do you know Danny Zuko?" Hannah said. "The movie ran in the seventies about a group of high school greasers set in the fifties."

"Duh, Mom—*Grease*, the movie with John Travolta, is a classic!"

Hannah smiled. Of course. What did she think? That her daughter was living in a bubble? Sometimes she wondered.

"Still, that movie came out twenty-two years before you were born."

"Well, it was about *your* time, right? I mean, the fifties."

"Not exactly" Hannah smiled, swirling the chocolate and vanilla flavors of her yogurt together. "I was just a baby then. My time was the seventies. Bell-bottoms, anti-war protests, David Cassidy."

"David *who?*"

Hannah chuckled. "I know that *ancient* pop culture is not your thing, but how can you not know about *The Partridge Family?*"

Olivia smacked her lips, tossing her mother a *look*. "Well, I could challenge you to a name-that-Kardashian trivia game, or an emoji game smackdown—and I'd *own* it!"

"No doubt, my lovely." Hannah laughed. She adored her brilliant and beautiful daughter with her glistening auburn hair and smooth, ivory skin. She had grown into a stunning fifteen-year-old, and had, it seemed, inherited the strong, solid features that both she and Broderick shared from Peter's Polish and Irish heritage. The only difference being that she had Hannah's pensive gray-blue eyes—just the same as her Grandmother Charlotte. Additionally, Olivia had Hannah's determination and never had to make anyone guess what she was thinking. That was one of the many things that Hannah loved about her. So, when the moment came to shift the conversation to the situation at hand, Hannah dove right in.

"I wanted to talk to you about what is going on right now, at home, I mean," Hannah said.

Olivia's body language suggested that she did not, as she crossed her arms. Still, she managed, "I know, Mom."

"*Know?* What do you know, sweetheart?" Hannah's breath caught in her throat.

"That you and Dad are splitting up," she said it as simply, as if she was talking about a movie that she had seen, or a TV show plot-line.

"How do you know this?" Hannah hedged, careful to not lead her daughter's response.

"I have eyes, that's all. I can see that he is never around. He never has been, really. It's just the way its always been. As long as I can remember."

"Why do you think that is?"

Olivia tossed her yogurt cup, unfinished, into the trash. "I dunno. He's not happy, I think." Then, she painfully looked her mother in the eye and said, "Are you?"

Hannah sighed. "No. Neither of us have really been happy for a long time. I am just a bit surprised that you were able to pick up on that. I'm sorry that you didn't get the best of us. It's—what do you call it? An epic fail."

Olivia rolled her eyes. "Please don't ever say that. And don't feel bad. Do you think that I am the only teenager whose parents are going through this? Really, it is what it is."

Hannah was taken aback. How was it that her scholarly daughter who excelled so much in math and science could be so sure of matters of relationships and human nature? That was her area of expertise!

"I just don't want you to worry about me, Mom. I am going to be fine, whatever you guys decide to do."

"Even with us going our separate ways?" Hannah hedged. "You'll be splitting your time between the two of us."

"Like I said, I just want you both to be happy—whatever that means for each of you."

Hannah, for once, was rendered speechless. What more was there to say? Any worry or fear that she might have had about her daughter's need to deal with the inevitable, was assayed. Unless, of course, she was pretending. The Murphys for certain and apparently, the Courtlands, were known for their tendency to hide the truth.

"I'm going to believe you, honey. But I want you to know that if ever you want to talk about this, or if anything happens that you are not okay with, I want you to let me know, okay?"

"Deal," she said and shouldered her vintage macramé cross-body bag. "Let's go check out the second-hand music shop. I hear that they have LPs. How cool is that?"

Hannah smiled. Her precious daughter definitely had an old soul, indeed. She only hoped that it was as resilient as it was beautiful.

CHAPTER 47
★ ★ ★

MAY 19th

HE SAT IN THE BACK of the class, staring at the threads fraying on the sleeve of his hoodie, which he wore in the August heat, waiting for the bell to ring. A pair of baggy jeans, a black T-shirt, and heavy combat-style boots completed his *I-don't-give-a-fuck* look. He had folded his freakishly tall frame into the steel and plywood desk, his russet-brown hair gelled on top of his head into spiked cowlicks and shaved liberally in the back close to his skull and around his enormously protruding ears. A gangly one hundred twenty pounds, he was stick-thin and would never be mistaken for being an athlete. In fact, he hated the cock-sucking bastards. The painful-looking acne on his face crept into an angry rash line snaking around to the back of his neck. It was heaviest on his cheeks and forehead—a grease slick mess of hot, swollen welts and oozy whiteheads ready to burst, just like him.

He had one jagged brow, where a self-piercing went bad. He had switched to the other side, where he had better luck, courtesy of a safety pin. Blackheads dotted the bridge of his nose and his lower lip, which was also pierced with a single stud. He wore Gothic-looking rings on nearly every finger, and heavy chains jutted from an actual leather dog collar around his neck. His fingernails were gnawed to the quick; every other one blackened with a Sharpie. Now, he was using it to doodle blood-dripping images of dragons on the leg of his shredded jeans. Beneath his tattered sleeves, he had track marks across his forearms, from when he regularly used to carve himself up with a razor, back when he was twelve. On his left forearm was his proudest work—an infinity symbol in which was displayed his eternal affection for Melissa Gates, a cheerleader with the prettiest smile he had ever seen. He had used his dad's hunting knife for the handiwork. It bled for three straight days and hurt like a mother, but then healed up nicely into a perfectly raised red scar. It was his badge of eternal devotion, which he would share with his beloved just in time for summer break. They would have the warm days and nights together with no distractions. He would let her into his world.

His darting brown eyes watched the minutes tick away to the hour mark.

The bell finally sounded, and he bolted from the desk to join the sea of students in the hall. He spotted Melissa immediately as she approached her locker with a gaggle of giddy cohorts. Her blonde highlights fell in swirling layers around her heart-shaped face and grazed the tops of her tan shoulders. She flashed a fifty-watt pageant smile. In a moment, she would find it—the note he had left for her tucked into her locker. It was unimaginative, but would prove to be the surest way to see if she felt the same. He had poured piety and loving words into the prose, asking her to meet him at the fountain in the park that evening. Then, he included his number so they could connect. It would be a simple request that would award him the opportunity to talk with her—alone, away from the others with their bourgeoisie mentality and materialistic pursuits. He was transcendent, and he was certain that Melissa was too. He knew it like he knew most things. She was the one singled out for him and, together, they would walk in the light. All she would need to do would be to say yes.

He watched from a safe distance as she opened her locker and the note fell out onto the floor. She picked it up and looked around, a bit perplexed. Then she slipped it into her folder.

He twitched nervously. It was about to happen. Everything he had hoped for.

CHAPTER 48
★ ★ ★

MELISSA GATES WAS A JEHOVAH'S Witness. She
lived with her father, Sebastian, who was a loving,
simple man, who lived in fear of his own shadow ever
since his wife died in a tragic accident five years prior.
Melissa needed to be for him wife, mother, and daughter
when it came to running the household and keeping her
dear father from drinking himself to death from a guilty
heart. He never forgave himself for not being able to save
his wife when a thug gunned her down in a botched rob-
bery on her way to make the bank deposit for the beauty
salon that she owned and ran. He found her, sprawled on
the sidewalk next to the parking lot in a pool of blood, her
hands still clutching the now-empty moneybag. The cops
had said that the killing was unintentional, the work of a
befuddled junkie.

Time had done little to ease the pain for either of them,
but Melissa, remarkably, had managed to rejoin the land
of the living and stepped up to console and care for her
despondent father. Now, as a junior in high school, it was

all that she could do to keep up the house, help with the business, and maintain her grades—all at the same time.

When a mysterious and misguided boy expressed his feelings for her in a hand-written note shoved in her locker, it only reinforced her need to be truthful with him. Eric Johansson was not her type, and she would never waste her time and energy in encouraging his kind, with his brooding and outcast ways that other girls might find tantalizing or dangerous. All it spelled out for her was T-R-O-U-B-L-E. She would ignore the misguided advance and hope that he would get the message.

"I'm going out, Daddy," Melissa said as she bent to kiss her father's grizzly cheek. He was ensconced in his La-Z-Boy recliner for the night, already popping open beer number three. "Dinner's on the stove. Don't wait up. I have to go in to the beauty shop to help Carmella shampoo, and then I'm meeting some friends from school for a bite."

The disheveled man nodded and gave a little grunt, patting her hand. "Okay, Princess."

She jumped into her relic '90s Accord, which at over a hundred thousand miles had more up-and-go than she could ever ask for in a vintage ride. She lowered the windows to let the warm evening breeze toss her hair as the radio blared FM tunes.

Her first client was Mrs. Jenkins—a fixture in the beauty shop for her once-a-week shampoo and style standing appointment. She was an older black matron who knew everyone—and everything about everyone—in the community. Melissa thought she reminded her of the woman in a short story she read in English class, named Miss Strangeworth, who was a busybody of sorts and who terrorized her neighbors with "kindness." But Mrs. Jenkins was nothing like that. Her intentions were pure and everyone loved her and sought her often-sage advice. There was not an evil bone in her body.

"What's new, sugar?" the old woman asked, beaming

with not-from-these-parts, southern charm. Originally from Alabama, the woman's accent had not faded a lick during the twenty-year span she had lived in Harrisburg.

Melissa helped her into the chair and adjusted the plastic gown's grip around her broad neck. "Not much, Mrs. Jenkins. Just trying to make it to summer break."

"Oh, you kids must be so excited. How's the cheerleading going?"

"We're done for the season, but we'll get together over the break to practice in the gym."

"Got any other summer plans?" she asked, removing her wire frames and leaning back into the shampoo bowl.

"I'm graduating next fall, so I suppose I'll be working on those college applications." Melissa winked, helping Mrs. Jenkins settle in and turning on the water jets. "Tell me if this is too warm."

Minutes later, Melissa had wrapped Mrs. Jenkins's head with a tight turban and moved her to the stylist's chair.

"Any prospects on your dance card, I mean?" the old woman pried quite unabashedly.

Melissa demurred. "Well, we'll have to see about that. If I can avoid attracting the Emo-types that look like they are straight out of *The Rocky Horror Picture Show*."

"Is that like those Goth kids who like wearing all black?" Mrs. Jenkins asked.

"Worse. They are in a league of their own. They think they're so dope, but I'm not into that just-got-out-of-a-coffin look."

Mrs. Jenkins guffawed. "You just keep holdin' out for that Mr. Right. I know he's out there looking for you. Make him wait, I say. It won't do him any harm!"

Melissa smiled and patted the woman on the back. "You wait here for Sylvia, now. She will make you look straight-fire gorgeous! Nice seeing you, Mrs. Jenkins."

Just then Melissa's phone buzzed. There was no Caller ID, so she let it go to voice mail. It was six thirty-five, and she had two more clients before she could go meet up with her friends.

When evening had fallen, Eric had showed up at the fountain to find that Melissa was not there. He first thought the worst—that something must have happened to detain her. He decided that he would wait. When eight o'clock rolled around, he began to grow uneasy, and finally, at ten p.m., he straddled his mountain bike and pedaled home in the dark.

Once in his room, he clicked away at his screen, bypassing the anti-government activist sites and militia group chat rooms, which he frequented under an alias and settled on a Facebook profile featuring Melissa's smiling face. An IM chimed on his screen, causing his heart to jump, but it was only a right-wing skinhead named Deeter with a litany of scores to settle with big government and the corporate pigs that continue to rape and ruin the country. Eric regularly "liked" his posts and comments, but had other things on his mind tonight. He clicked off the site and dialed Melissa once again from a masked number that he had hacked with a few well-placed strokes of the keyboard months earlier. He didn't want her to know that had her direct number. He needed *her* to call him first. If she answered, he would know that she was indeed all right. The line rang, and then bounced to voice mail once again.

I'll wait until tomorrow and find out what happened, he told himself. Then, he proceeded to pore over his many pictures of her taken from the yearbook and school paper, which he had arranged and then rearranged on his wall near the closet. His favorite was one of her in her cheerleading outfit, beaming, with arms outstretched and pom-poms high in the air at the top of a three-person pyramid. She looked so pure and radiant.

When he bored of that, he began clicking around the Internet for some advice that might help him with courting Melissa. He Googled the term "soul mate" and the algorithms delivered ten links to articles and reviews for a syndicated radio talk show shrink who simply went by the name of "Dr. Hannah." She was, among other things, a relationships expert. Her radio show, *Straight Talk with Dr. Hannah*, seemed legit.

He clicked on her publicity photo. The image of a middle-aged woman with golden-blonde hair and a pearl choker beamed with arms crossed confidently in the headshot. She seemed to have a kind face. He sat up the rest of the night downloading her books and listening to sound bites of her show from her website. Although skeptical, he concluded that she might be able to help him—*it was worth a try.*

CHAPTER 49
★ ★ ★

THE NEXT DAY, WHEN ERIC approached Melissa Gates on the front steps of the gymnasium, she acted cool and aloof. She was uncharacteristically alone, but wouldn't be for long, so he had to move fast. "Hey," he said in a casual tone unmatched by his stormy, agitated eyes. "You didn't show up yesterday."

"Oh, yeah," she stammered. "I am sorry about that. Um, it's *Eric*, right? I am sorry, but I am sort of seeing someone," she said, which in effect, was not completely untrue. She had eyes for the incredibly handsome linebacker, Grant Leary, and word around school was that he liked her too. Besides, this one creeped her out in more ways than she could count.

A dwarf of a girl with Juicy Couture sunglasses and a ponytail rushed up to Melissa, squealing about concert tickets at the pavilion and pulled Melissa away. They quickly started walking in the opposite direction toward the main building and a group of upperclassmen who were joining in a cryptic huddle. "Thanks anyway!" Melissa called over her shoulder, walking swiftly, her cheer skirt flipping in the wind.

Eric stood glued to the steps, scarcely able to process what had just happened. He watched, as moments later, Grant Leary, a jock-ass prick, bounded up to Melissa like a baboon and started to say and do things that made her toss her hair and laugh.

Eric's blood rose to a full boil. Hot with rage, he ran home, pulverizing the ground with his heavy boots. He kicked closed his bedroom door and rammed his fist clear through the wall on which the picture of Melissa was tacked, causing the plaster to splinter.

An hour later, he blew up her phone with a series of texts and calls, but she didn't pick up. He could only stare at her small static image on his Facebook wall, still waiting for her to confirm his repeated friend requests, which went unanswered—ignored; even under the multiple alias accounts he had created. She was icing him out, for sure. In fact, he thought, growing further agitated, she was probably with the Neanderthal jock-prick at that very moment, both lusting for each other, no doubt. She was not unlike the others, after all—every last one of them with their hedonistic, worldly pursuits.

Minutes passed, and he began to rage. He should have never doubted the voices that told him different.

This, he vowed, would cost them. But it would take planning. He did a quick search on the web, which took only seconds to land pay dirt. A guy named "Chucky" knew exactly what it would take to get the job done.

Eric grinned, settling into the pull and bidding of the mission. He had all that he would need to set the wheels in motion—and he had nothing but time.

CHAPTER 50
★ ★ ★

JULY 2015
(TWO MONTHS LATER)

T HE FIRST LETTER HAD ARRIVED in the mail in early July. It was addressed to *The Dr. Hannah Show*. The production assistant, Tatum, received it along with a stack of business correspondence addressed to the station and put the unopened envelope into Hannah's mail slot with all the others.

It was not until the next day that Jon Novotny sliced it open. It was post-marked from Manhattan on June 28th, and had no return address. The paper was torn from a spiral college-ruled notebook and handprinted. Scrawled at the top in red ink, the nonsensical text read:

Dr. Hannah,

They don't see me or think the way that I do. I watch them move and it disgusts me. They are weak because they don't cry like they should. They go on just laughing . . . I wait and imagine what I know to be true, that no one else does. One day, they will all BURN and it will be MY TURN TO FLY!

~ EJ

Jon was regularly screening listener correspondence for usable show material for a reoccurring segment called "Hannah's Mail Bag," as he did daily. The batch was typically filled with strange and often compelling correspondence from listeners asking for help; others denouncing Hannah's unorthodox methods of therapy and high- moral route to well-being. All types of people wrote in to the show: fanatics, anarchists, naysayers, believers, beloved fans, saints as well as sinners, and the like. These penned, faxed, texted, and emailed their thoughts, questions and comments to the radio station daily. It was Jon's job to weed through the chaff to find the cards, letters, and emails worthy of becoming show material. The rest were relegated to the public files for storage by order of the FCC, for public viewing if desired. The real bizarre ones, the "nut cases," as Jon affectionately referred to them, he filed in a special folder marked, MIXED NUTS.

Jon re-read the letter and simply shook his head. He attached a yellow post-it note to the front, on which he wrote in black marker, "EJ." Then, he added it to the NUTS file folder and returned it to his desk drawer.

He decided not to bother Hannah with mention of it.

Four weeks later, EJ had earned his own folder, and the hand-written letters began coming at an average of two to three per week, only, as the weeks progressed, the postmarks varied, and the content had become more disturbing in nature, resembling dark, rambling poetic verse:

I dream of them falling, one by one-- See them dancing off my gun. I shoot them as they run. WHY WON'T ANYONE HEAR ME?

EJ also occasionally emailed Hannah's "fan" account with disturbing text. Jon had noted that on the most recent email, to Dr. Hannah just that morning, he lamented:

WHY HAVEN'T YOU WRITTEN ME BACK? AREN'T YOU

SUPPOSED TO CARE? MAYBE YOU THINK YOU ARE BENEATH
LISTENING TO US NON-JEWS . . . ARE YOU A BIGOT, DOC?
SHAME ON YOU!

Jon's pulse quickened as he printed out the jarring text.
He did not like the tone of this one and feared that EJ was
growing more agitated and impatient. Ignoring him was
only proving to incite his eccentric nutcase brain. It was
time, Jon reasoned, to share the letters with Hannah. She
would, of course, be furious that he had withheld them
from her. She was like that about such things, rightfully
cautious when it came to dealing with the general public
at large, but fearless in the face of psychosis. That was what
made her *Dr. Hannah*.

The other hurdle would be Allison. She did not like to
be kept in the dark about anything.

CHAPTER 51
★ ★ ★

AUGUST 2015

"HOW LONG DID YOU SAY that he has been send-ing them?"

"About six weeks now."

"Six weeks!" Hannah's mouth opened in disbelief.

They were all gathered around the large conference room table: Hannah, Jon, Allison, Stan Newhall, the program director, and Don Brockett from legal. Allison clutched her last working stress ball. She had annihilated the previous dozen she had stowed away in her office drawer. She was furious with the position that Jon had put her in, namely, being out-of-the-know and looking inept in front of her team. Earlier that morning she had given Jon the riot act behind closed doors, in which she colorfully ripped him a new one. "You idiot! You leave me no choice but to stand there with my dick in my hand, unaware, while this *Whack-job* is sending cryptic manifestos to my number one show host."

Jon apologized, but felt the need to protect Hannah more than his own job, so he took the tongue-lashing and braced for the next tidal wave to come—Hannah's reaction to the news.

Marney was in Boston and could not attend the meeting; it was just as well, as she was the biggest alarmist of them all when it came to Hannah's safety.

The ominous manila file folder sat warily in the center of the conference table. The contents, some twenty-three letters—all hand-written with no return address—had been mailed from various boroughs in New York. They were, however, all from the same ominous mysterious anti-fan simply called EJ.

Hannah could not hide her concern. She riffled through the stack while everyone watched, riveted. She chose one at random and held up the tattered page and read it aloud. Her voice was smooth and flawless in the delivery:

"Damn the makers of the code; the voices who try to tell us who we are. Redfish sings of sweet release to prisoners of Bremen's Halls – his trilogy is my shield. A song of seven swirling swords . . . "

She handed the letter to Jon, who was sitting on her right. "I don't get it. What's with the riddles? What's this guy trying to say?" she asked the room.

Jon was only able to wag his head with the rest of them.

"And who the hell is this Redfish?" Don asked the sea of blank stares.

Much to everyone's surprise, Hannah offered clarification. "He's a head-banger from a heavy metal band called Code X. My daughter is banned from listening to their CDs, but some of her friends do. Redfish is a fascist lunatic with a sick mind and a recording contract, which makes him double-dangerous."

Everyone stirred and shifted in their seats.

Stan Newhall concurred. He, too, had a teenager. "Yeah, they claim that their music is nothing more than teen angst—senseless ballads blaring from iPods and smart-phones. Some call it commercialism, but there's a fine line between performance art and propaganda. Anyway, this Redfish guy, particularly—he's the son of Satan—on an *off* day. He's clearly unhinged."

Allison twitched. It was a telltale sign of supreme annoyance. Inside, a volcano was bubbling. The more she heard, the more the lava churned.

Hannah's mind was spinning. She painfully rubbed her temples. "So is this a threat, or what?" she asked no one in particular.

Don Brockett lunged forward. "Give the letters and emails to me. I want to look them over."

"No." Hannah seized the file before he could grab it. "I want them. Every last one. They're written to me, are they not?"

Jon winced.

Hannah insisted, "I've got this."

Allison hedged, "I don't like the looks of this at all, Hannah. Why don't you let Don take the letters and review them? I've had a chance to examine only a few, but from what I've seen, I'd say that this guy is off his meds, all right." Then, she added quickly, "But realize, folks—no actual threat has been waged. Let's keep an eye on things a little while longer." Then, turning to Jon, "You let me know what, if anything, changes. Meanwhile, Hannah, there's no need for you to concern yourself here. We'll keep you posted."

Hannah sat, deflated, as Allison took the file from in front of Hannah and tucked it beneath her beefy arm.

Hannah didn't want to put the station in jeopardy, especially with the changes coming with the extended syndication of her show and the pending contract deal with Global Network. Too much was at stake. Jon should have never called the meeting. He should have brought the letters to her attention privately first. She was so annoyed with him she could have screamed. Instead, she smiled valiantly through her veneers.

"That's all, then," Allison concluded and everyone rose from their chairs. That was it. Case closed.

Hannah grabbed Jon's sleeve as he started for the door and whispered quite compellingly into his ear, squeezing his arm for emphasis with each word. "I want copies of every last one of those letters on my desk ASAP."

The file appeared on Hannah's desk within the hour. Tatum, who had been sworn to secrecy by Jon, and at his request, had copied every last one without Allison knowing. Hannah placed the file into her Birkin bag and waltzed out of the radio station with no one the wiser.

She proceeded to cancel her afternoon hair appointment, called Adelita to have Olivia picked up from volleyball practice before dinner, and switched her phone to silent. She purchased the tallest and strongest latte that the coffee shop in the Flats had on tap and took a small table near the window, overlooking the river, where any number of barges and freighters could be seen gliding by, along with smaller boats pulling into the port for refueling.

Hannah put on her Cartier readers and bent over the file and got to work, scrutinizing each disturbing letter—every last one of them with mounting distress, as the air-horns from the boats sounded off the water.

CHAPTER 52
★ ★ ★

AUGUST 11. 2015

ERIC WAS GETTING TIRED OF waiting. Six weeks had gone by, and the radio bitch had not mentioned a single one of his letters on the air! He had been listening each day to her show on his headphones, glued to the bed, staring up at a picture of Melissa Gates torn from the yearbook and plastered on his ceiling. A photo of Grant Leary lay mutilated in the trash bin. The radio shrink never chose *his* problems to discuss, did she? It was always one other lame predicament or another set forth by a babbling, bored housewife with a prescription addiction or a disillusioned left-wing millennial with a cell phone, a corporate job, and a ton of student debt, contending with the guilt of an inner-office affair.

He scrawled in his journal, a messy tirade:

Damn the life of the working man's man who sees his reality shrinking, stinking, with each micro chip . . . another year goes by. This is why he must die and take the worldly rages for his own sins . . . .

He closed his eyes tightly as his fingers dug into the
cover of the notebook, breaking the skin, leaving drop-
lets of smudgy blood imprints around the margins. His
twisted prose was all there, along with a list of dates, mark-
ing the events with no particular distinction that separated
the litany of triumphs from the tragedies: *Two thousand
eleven—January 8ᵗʰ, Arizona Congresswoman Gabrielle Gif-
fords shot along with twelve others at a public appearance in
Casas Adobes, Arizona; May 22, an EF-5 tornado hits Joplin,
Missouri, killing one hundred and sixty-one people and leaving
one thousand injured; April 29, the Royal Wedding of Prince
William and Catherine Middleton in the United Kingdom. Two
thousand twelve—April 4, re-election of Barack Obama; October
22, Hurricane Sandy hits the East Coast, killing two hundred
people; December 14, Sandy Hook Elementary School shooting
in Newtown, Connecticut, killing twenty children and six adult
staff members; shooter also kills his mother; commits suicide; Two
thousand thirteen—April 15, Boston Marathon Bombings, killing three and injuring two hundred sixty-four; May 20, an EF-5
tornado hits Moore, Oklahoma, killing fifty-one people, twenty of
them children, injuring two hundred thirty. Two dozen schoolchil-
dren trapped beneath rubble.*
He studied the list with a vapid, dark resolve.

Whenever he did leave the house it was to stalk and
follow his prey. Little did Melissa and Grant know that
everywhere they went—to the movie theater, the mall, and
the local coffee shop—Eric was following them. Watching.
He could have been an ordinary fifteen-year-old boy in
every way, just enjoying the summer break, with his ball
cap pulled low, earbuds encircling his neck, and a graphic
novel protruding from his jeans pocket. But this was not

the case. Something else was there, deep behind his flat brown eyes, where dark and evil thoughts resided and made their way into a tattered journal in which he poured out his thoughts and plans and cataloged his lists. Where he drafted his poems and riddles before sending them out into the ether. There, where he spilled his thoughts, first onto the page and then into real life. There was something that betrayed the new outward persona he tried to project, staying just below the radar. It was the strange, incessant voices in his head that assured him that he too had the power to somehow change the world. *Were they all too stupid to see the truth?* he wondered.

No matter. It was nearly time.

CHAPTER 53
★ ★ ★

HANNAH RETURNED HOME, EXHAUSTED. SHE ran a bath, staring at the foaming water pensively. Peter had already been gone for nearly six months, but in many ways, it seemed longer. All he had wanted to tell her three months prior at the restaurant was that he was going to stay permanently in Pittsburgh due to Anthony's failing health condition. He had said that he was not ready to tell the children the truth yet. That he would do it in his own time. Further, he was not sure that it would be in the best interest for Olivia to be exposed to his lifestyle, considering all that was going on. *That* was an understatement, as far as Hannah was concerned. They would have to amend the visitation agreement on the divorce decree and transfer full custody to Hannah, in which Olivia would be allowed to remain in her normal schedule for school, home, and extracurricular activities until Peter's life would be in order and he could be the father that she needed him to be. It would be up to Hannah to smooth things out, and try to help Olivia understand what was going on and why her father would not be taking her on his visitation weekends—for now.

As expected, Olivia had taken the initial news like a trooper and said little, although Hannah knew that her daughter's heart was broken. It was just like Peter to leave the messes for her to clean up, to fix things. However, all the new clothes, latest gadgets, and fancy vacations could not begin to put the family back together again. This was indeed the one thing that Hannah was unable to remedy, or would ever be able to.

This was not a typical Friday night. Blissfully, the house was completely hers. Olivia was spending the night at her girlfriend Meghan's, and Adelita had the night off.

Hannah soaked languidly in the steamy hot bath, letting the warmth seep into her bones. She actually ached in places she never knew possible—deep in the crevices of her back and neck, a tension was racking her tiny five-foot-two frame with gridlock.

She smoothed the fragrant suds into her wet skin; the bath smelled like a Caribbean dream of pineapples and coconut. It had been months since she had taken a vacation. Maybe she would take Marney's advice and whisk herself and Olivia off somewhere warm and tropical, before the school year started and her new hosting job with Global Network would bind her to endless wardrobe fittings, promotional obligations, and tapings. It would do them both some good. Maybe they could even invite the boys as well—Ty, Sara, and the twins too—making it a *whole* family get-away. She could book them a couple of suites in San Luca or Costa Rica. She then sighed as the idea faded. It would take far more than aromatherapy or daydreams to organize such an excursion. The truth being, she just wasn't free to up and go anymore. Besides, everyone in the extended family was busy with his or her own lives.

She closed her eyes tightly. There were so many obligations and so many unanswered questions that continued to plague her. For one, *who was behind the mystery emails and letters? And why did this EJ single her out?*

She had deduced from much of the content that the writer was most probably not an adult. The music references and grammatical errors suggested a teenager or adolescent, but might have been intentional to throw her off. Hannah had received enough mail from pre-teens to recognize the thought patterns and rationales; yet, this one was different—very disturbing in so many ways. The writer was most definitely reaching out, calling attention to his dissatisfaction with authority. Why, if he was truly seeking her help, didn't he just ask for it? It was puzzling, all right, and she knew that it would be better not to engage with him.

Still, flashes of the twisted verse floated through her mind . . . *the faces of Bremen's Hall will fall and blood will pay for Redfish's Day in streaming glory. Be ready!*

Hannah climbed in bed and slipped into a deep, restless sleep. She dreamt of horrid, frightening creatures with large fish-heads and spiked fins chasing her in a labyrinth of hallways—every turn producing closed doors and shuttered windows; brick embankments and cold steel cabinets . . . *"cabinets with a code . . . number to number . . . name to name, before the bell they will all go up in flames!"*

Hannah sat up in bed with a jolt. The images she saw in her dream were as clear as day. *Cabinets with a code!* She was certain that her gut instinct was spot-on, and that her interpretation of the poem might be true—the picture was growing clearer by the moment.

"He's talking about lockers, like in a *school*."

She raced to the office the next morning and met Jon at his cubicle before he had a chance to fill his mug with the usual jolt of one-hundred-watt Novotny java made from three packets of industrial grounds and a hint of coca powder. It had been raining all night, and the office was emptier than usual.

"Hey!" she said brightly. "I brought you one . . . a *real* one from a coffee shop—tall, hot, and full of octane. Can't have a good show without a hot mic, right?" She chuckled nervously and produced two Starbucks coffees and plopped one on his desk and started right in. "I need you to do me a little favor, Jon."

"Bribery. I like it!" He smiled.

She opened the tattered file folder with the letters from EJ and spread them onto the desk. Jon noticed that many of the pages had been marked with yellow highlighter and blue ink. "Now," Hannah began, arranging them in some sort of meaningful order, "I have reviewed each of these carefully, and I think I found some definite clues to substantiate my theory."

Jon stared at her blankly. "Your *what?*"

Hannah went on. "Our psycho-guy . . . he's a *kid.* A kid with a real problem, that's what I think. Only, I'm afraid from the sound of it, that he's planning on taking out some sort of vengeance on himself—or others."

Jon's eyes widened. "You think . . . ?"

"Could be, Jon. I don't know. And can we take the chance of not finding out?" She adjusted her designer frames further down her nose and looked over them. "There are still so many damn unanswered questions. His poems are filled with threatening innuendo. What is *The Day of Atonement?* Who is *Melissa?* And where on earth is *Bremen's Hall* that he refers to?"

"That's easy," Jon said, switching on his computer and clicking away as she spoke.

"I think this kid is more than serious, Jon. He's obviously reaching out to me for some reason. I'd be remiss if I didn't try to do something, right? And if—"

"Holy shit!"

"What?"

Jon was gawking dumbly at the screen in disbelief. She

leaned in over his shoulder. "What is it?"

"Well, it looks as though we're not going to have to hunt down the junior terrorist after all. He just sent his next correspondence to your personal email. The return address is: EJ2000@aol.com."

Jon scooted over to let Hannah sit down. She shuffled the mouse across the pad and began clicking to open the document. Finally, the message appeared: NICE TO SEE YOU – BITCH! I'M STILL HERE . . . WAITING FOR YOUR REPLY. THE DAYS DRAW NEAR. THE MASSES WILL GATHER AND FILL BREMEN'S HALL WITH HOMEGE. REDFISH EVER REIGNS AND SWEET, SWEET MELISSA WILL SOON KNOW MY NAME, BUT WILL YOU?

Hannah paled.

"I'll call security. He's too close for comfort now, speaking to you like this!" Jon reached for the phone.

"No! Don't—please! Don't tell anyone about this. If Allison finds out I've been threatened, she'll send me far away for safe-keeping, someplace like a long vacation in the Himalayas. Not a *word* to anyone, you understand? Please, just let me handle this. I promise, it's going to be all right. No one is going to bully anyone, and no one is going to get hurt. Okay?"

Jon nodded, wondering how in the world she could be so sure. He was unconvinced.

"I promise, Jon . . . trust me," she reassured. "I've got this."

"What are you going to do?"

"I'm going to respond. It's what he wants, isn't it?"

She clicked on the reply icon and tapped away at the keys haphazardly, nervously missing the fine points of capitalization, periods, and commas. WHERE ARE YOU, EJ? I AM READY TO LISTEN IF YOU WANT TO TALK. I AM SORRY IF YOU ARE ANGRY WITH ME. YOU CAN TALK TO ME NOW IF YOU LIKE. WHERE DO YOU LIVE? WRITE ME BACK AND LET'S CHAT

ABOUT WHATEVER YOU'D LIKE. OKAY?

She sent the string of words in what truly felt like a futile attempt to toss a book on swimming lessons to a drowning man. Within minutes, the network alert message popped onto the screen, indicating quite officially that the message sent from Hannah's terminal to EJ2000@ aol.com was *undeliverable*. His email account had been disabled.

CHAPTER 54
★ ★ ★

FRIDAY, AUGUST 14TH

IT HAD BEEN A STRESSFUL several months for Hannah, and it was about to feel even more like she was living someone else's life. She was in a whirlwind of change. It all became real when earlier that summer, she had flown out to meet with Bumpy Friedman himself and enjoyed a delightful lunch with him, his staff, and his talented writers after being given a tour of the studio and a rundown of their vision for the talk show. She and Marney had attended the meeting, with Marney staying on another few days to iron out the particulars for the final contract, which would be signed ceremoniously by all four show hosts right there at Global Studios on the twenty-first of August, officially cementing the deal.

Hannah was exhausted. She needed to prepare not only for the big signing session, but also for a huge promotional photo shoot that was slated for two weeks after that back at Global Studios with the entire cast. She hadn't begun to imagine what she was going to pack or wear for the high-profile events. It was hard to believe that it would all be set in motion in just one short week.

In spite of everything, Hannah was excited and knew that the challenges ahead were ones that she had been preparing for all of her life. She was going to change so many lives. And she couldn't wait to get started.

That evening, following her show, Hannah begged off a production meeting with Jon and the crew, even though it was tradition that on Tuesdays, the meeting was followed religiously by an hour of socializing and winding down over a couple of cold ones at City Scape just up the street. Instead, she caught an earlier flight home. She missed Olivia something awful and just wanted to spend some time with her. She had planned the details of their entire weekend. Hair braiding, watching Netflix marathons, and eating endless bowls of popcorn. Olivia was growing up so fast. Nothing else rejuvenated Hannah's soul more then to just chill with her beautiful, amazing daughter.

Together, they would also make their bi-weekly visit to the nursing home to see Charlotte. It was hard to believe that she had been there eighteen years, well before Olivia was born. Regrettably, Olivia had never gotten to know her grandmother, nor could remember her grandfather, Robert, who had passed away in the summer of 2006, when Olivia was just six years old, and right when Hannah's career was about to take full flight. Hannah felt extremely guilty that somehow her dear mother, who now could not recognize any of her family members, or dress or feed herself, was left to linger in a state of anxiety and delusion. The only solace being that on good days, she still called out Robert's name and seemed to be conversing with him for hours on end in contented lucidity. This, for Hannah, was a blessing that only her dear deceased father could have brought to his eternal bride.

"Who are you talking to?" Hannah would ask, stroking

her mother's knotted and vein-riddled hands folded languidly atop her lap.

"Him," she would say with a watery smile. "Lieutenant Colonel Robert Courtland. He says that the baby . . . is crying."

"Look who's here," Hannah would say, motioning for Olivia to lean in.

"Hi, Grandma," Olivia would say, softly and sweetly to the vacant blue eyes.

"Oh, hello," would come the startled reply.

And then Olivia would brush her grandmother's silver hair as long as she would allow her to, while Charlotte sat in silence. Together, they would color beautiful bluebirds from her coloring book, and then Olivia would tape them up on the walls of Charlotte's room.

These were beautiful, bittersweet exchanges when a beat would pass and then Charlotte would once again ask, "Are you going to take me home?"

"In a little while, Mom. Why don't you rest a bit for now?"

So went the exchange that was stuck on repeat like a song in one's head, or a gif on perpetual replay. Flashes of Hannah's mother were ever present, though, in the unspoken bond that no illness or disease could erase, day after day. Year after year. It was all that they had, and in the end, it would have to be enough.

When it was time to leave, Hannah would watch Olivia select a housedress for her grandmother to wear the next day and lay it out on the chair, often tucking a sticker or a little love note in the pocket for her to find. She'd hoped that it would make her grandmother smile. Hannah knew that the sweet, enduring spirit that made Olivia came from the finest souls in Charlotte and Robert. And that no matter what life would bring, she would be okay. They all would be.

CHAPTER 55
★ ★ ★

HE HAD BEEN CAREFUL, ALL right. He made sure
to buy the steel pipe and two end caps at different
stores and to dispose of the receipts. He got a fast, reliable
fuse at the hobby store. The moon-faced lady at the check-
out must have thought he was model rocket geek, or some
such. He flashed a fake smile and let her think whatever
she pleased.

He hurried home, locked his bedroom door, and turned
up his stereo. Code X wailed from the thumping speakers.
He donned rubber gloves, heeding the sagacious advice
gleaned from the internet tutorial: *NEVER handle the pipe
with your bare hands, or you'll go straight to jail—forensic science
will bust your ass on the real.*

He then proceeded to wash all of the pieces individu-
ally with rubbing alcohol on cotton balls that he got from
his mother's bathroom cabinet—especially tending to the
threads.

Next, he laid everything out on the carpet so that it
could dry thoroughly.

Then, he drilled a hole into one of the end caps for the
hobby shop fuse. He reread the instructions printed from a

screen shot: *If you want to make your own fuse, you can (carefully) do so by grinding up about 1000 white-head stick matches and gluing the granules to some durable cord. Be careful to give yourself a good six to eight inches of coating, or you're going to blow yourself to fucking pieces . . . HAHAHAHAAH!*

There was little anyone could ever do with Eric. He was a sullen, conflicted soul right from the womb, it seemed. Dora Johansson did her best to appease her finicky child, whose tantrums started well before he started preschool. He was distant and aloof most days, preferring to sulk away the hours tinkering with his cars and blocks alone in a corner rather than interact with other children. Throughout the years and with him being her and Wayne's only child, they searched for answers to help them to connect with their brooding and emotionally distant son.

By the time he had reached middle school, it became apparent that he was defiant and possibly even dangerous. School issues arose, and although there was nothing wrong with Eric's IQ—quite the contrary, he was quite brilliant—it was evident that he lacked social skills and graces that would serve him into high school and beyond. This, of course, was of great concern to Wayne Johansson, who had been recently placed in the position of Superintendent after a seventeen-year tenure climb from teacher to principal, to top-level administrator in the district.

Reprimanding Eric was pointless. Wayne and Dora frequently had resorted to taking his bedroom door off of the hinges so that he could not hole up in his room and refuse to come out to eat, bathe, or interact with the family. Each time they took it off, he would do just enough to earn it back and—for a while—appear to be okay and compliant. But this was always too short-lived, and more often than not, Eric's parents were prisoners in their own house that they shared with a boy whom they sometimes feared.

Wayne Johansson by no means considered himself the perfect specimen of humankind, but the information that burned its indelible mark into the bark of his family tree could not be denied and seemed to suggest something sinister and culpable. His Aunt Ruth had relayed the truth to him on his twenty-first birthday in October of 1991. She had just celebrated a birthday herself—her fiftieth—just two days prior, in which she felt the need to divulge a gargantuan "family secret" that had been burning in her bosom for decades. Together, they shared his first taste of whiskey—and the dark truth that had plagued their family since the beginning of the twentieth century.

Aunt Ruth had felt the need to unburden herself to her dear nephew, who, it seemed, deserved to know the truth about his heritage. With the new decade upon her and her newfound freedom from divorce number three, she no longer felt the need to hold the information under her hat.

"You know that our decedents were early settlers who came West from the Southern Appalachians before settling in rural Missouri, right?"

"Right," Wayne said, proud of his English and Scots-Irish ancestry said to be the lineage of one Theodore Johansson, his paternal great-grandfather.

"Yeah, well, our dear ole grandpappy did more than till the land. He married a child bride, Constance Johansson. She had that name because when she married him at the tender age of just sixteen—they were *first cousins.*"

Wayne's eyes widened, and he took another swig of the brown liquid. "Aren't we supposed to be one-fifth Native American as well?" he asked.

"That is also true, but for what I am about to tell you, you're going to need another swig of that fire water."

It seemed that Aunt Ruth was a whiz with genealogy

and had uncovered more than just dirt on the family gene pool. An exhaustive search through the archives and historical annals revealed a scandal that might have explained the litany of destruction and dysfunction that ran through the veins of the Johansson men for more than a century.

Ruth's words were haunting. "Your father—my brother—was holding a secret that he never even shared with your mother."

"How do you know that?" he had asked.

"Trust me," she'd said. "Caleb never shared it with a soul. He took it to his early grave when he took his life all those Christmases ago. You would never know any of this if I hadn't told you. Not even your Aunt June knows."

Wayne was uneasy. He had definitely had a strained relationship with his father through the years, but never really knew why. *What had his father hidden from all of them all these years?* He had to know, and poured a second shot of whiskey that would keep his dear aunt talking. She had since produced a large graphic that she had made from posterboard set out on the table before them.

"It is recorded that Theodore and Constance Johansson had four children between 1913 and 1919, the last born being a girl named Mary Kate. The only boy was named Arnell, your paternal grandfather. In 1937, at age twenty, Arnell married a young woman named Ann Marley. She was found murdered in their farmhouse, having been brutally dismembered with a chopping ax. Granddad Arnell had called the authorities, who found him weeping over the body with blood splattered on his coveralls and holding the ax, which he had taken down from the barn wall."

"*What!*" Wayne was incredulous.

"They arrested him for the murder," Aunt Ruth said coolly, and then continued. "Arnell pleaded guilty, citing childhood abuse at the hands of his father, Theodore Johansson, that caused him to do it. Further, Arnell had been accused, according to hearsay around the family camp, of having molested his baby sister, Mary Ellen, in her crib back in 1919, when she was just seven months old. Constance, it was said, banished him from the house and made the then-nine-year-old boy sleep in the barn for the remainder of his years, until he had come of age, and then he was sent on his way with a one-way train ticket north and three dollars tucked in his dungarees. They ostracized him and never spoke of the incident until years later, when the murder of Ann Marley occurred in Jefferson City."

She went on to explain how Arnell then did hard time at the Missouri State Penitentiary, where he dodged the new bill calling for execution by lethal gas due to a technicality. He was out on good behavior within ten years. Then, he married wife number two—Lorna Boothe, a seamstress from Kansas City. Together, they had three children—Wayne's father, Caleb, and the two girls, June and Ruth. According to a journal of which Aunt Ruth swore that she had obtained from Wayne's father directly, it was then-nine-year-old Caleb who had discovered his mother's body, which had been stabbed thirteen times at his father's hand with a kitchen knife, fatally severing her neck. Caleb had walked in unknowingly on his father frantically attempting to mop up the blood. They made eye contact, and then Caleb ran as fast as he could to the back of the house and locked himself in his parents' bedroom closet. Arnell, in a panic and rage, pounded on the door for him to come out and face his wrath, telling young Caleb that he would not live to tell what he had seen. "I'll smoke you out like a rat," he had heard his father say. And then all went quiet. He later learned that Arnell had gone back into the kitchen to fetch a box of matches. His heavy work boots pounded from the shed back to the house, and Caleb could remember hearing the sound of him pouring kerosene on all of the floorboards.

"That's when he reached above his head to the highest shelf there in the closet and felt for his father's shotgun,"

Aunt Ruth said matter-of-factly. "He knew where it was and could only pray that the bastard had it loaded."

When he heard his father approach the closet door, Caleb burst through and charged at him with the shotgun. He fired four times, stopping only when he saw Arnell fall to the floor. He dropped the gun and grabbed the matches.

Ruth leaned way in for emphasis. "He got both me and June out of the house into the backseat of the rusted Buick and then lit the fire that destroyed the house—and any evidence of the brutal murders that had occurred there."

Wayne was speechless, shocked and confused. "He just got behind the wheel and never looked back?" he said, rubbing his sweaty hands on his Lucky Brand jeans. He was trembling.

"Yep. He took us up the road to some relatives, who kept the secret that we were too young to know. Years later, he met your mother in Columbus. He never spoke of it, but it never left him, obviously," Aunt Ruth said, letting it all sink in. "For the longest time, your Aunt June and I thought that Aunt Mary and Uncle Charlie were our parents."

"This is all so unbelievable," Wayne said, struggling to digest the facts. "What is it? A family curse?"

"Worse," Ruth said, lighting up a Winston. "A curse of the worst kind—it's in the blood."

CHAPTER 56
★ ★ ★

IT WAS WEDNESDAY, TWO DAYS before the big sign-ing, and Hannah was finally ready. She had just finished the taping of her last radio show for the week and could now focus on the exciting weekend ahead of her. She had even promised Olivia that she could accompany her to the Big Apple for some fun mother/daughter bonding time on the weekend after her signing meeting. The two would go shopping at Bloomingdale's and enjoy some unabashed people watching in Times Square. She had booked the flight for both of them. Hannah had figured that missing one day of school would do little harm to her brilliant daughter's soaring GPA.

Before leaving the studio, Hannah checked her cell-phone, which had been turned off during her broadcast. There were a string of text messages from Peter. He had apparently been leaving messages all afternoon. She had presumed that it was regarding the last of the documents he had yet to sign to finalize the divorce. He had been dragging his feet, and it was not good for any of them to prolong the inevitable. This would be a part of her new start, as well moving forward. She would rather, she'd

decided, just refer him to her lawyer, Stuart Lanier. It was
the final step in the process, and frankly, Hannah was in no
frame of mind now to deal with it.

She deleted the backlog of messages, leaving them unanswered. Whatever it was, it could wait until Lanier was back
in his office in the morning. She tossed the phone back
into her Birkin and headed to the airport to go home.

When she pulled into the driveway sometime after eight
o'clock p.m., Adelita burst through the front door with
apron flailing, and pounded across the lawn, waving her
arms over her head.

"Missus! Oh, Missus! It's Doctor Murphy— he's been
calling all day to say—" She was out of breath and choking.
By the time she reached Hannah, she had to steady herself
against the hood of the Mercedes. Adelita was clearly too
large a woman to be sprinting across the grass. She was
shaken with the levity of her charge, which was to get this
message to Mrs. Murphy *at all costs*, having been rightfully
told that it was truly a matter of life and death.

"He say to come to Philadelphia right away! Please—it's
okay. You go . . . I stay with Olivia, no?"

"Philadelphia? Tonight? What on earth . . . ?"

Hannah glanced down at her phone. There were at least
fifteen text messages from Peter. One read: HANNAH –
ANTHONY IS SUFFERING BADLY. HE'S FAILING
FAST. PLEASE, I BEG OF YOU TO COME. I WILL
SIGN ALL PAPERS. GOD HELP ME, IT'S HAP-
PENING. I NEED YOU. I AM AT THE HERITAGE
CORNER INN. PLEASE!

Hannah could scarcely believe the timing. How could
he ask this of her? *Now?*

Adelita, who knew better than to pretend that she
understood, lowered her eyes. "Jus' go, Missus. Go! I take
care of things, *si*?"

All Hannah could think about was disappointing Olivia and their planned weekend. Perhaps she could fly her out on Saturday and meet up with her there instead. She would have to see. Either way, she vowed to make it up to her. She *had* to. And, she had to go.

In less than an hour, Hannah was packed and in an Uber Sedan bound for the airport, and flight two thirty-five to Philadelphia.

CHAPTER 57

★ ★ ★

PITTSBURGH, PA

HANNAH ARRIVED AT THE HOSPITAL in a cab. She came straight from the airport, rolling her travel bag behind her, packed for the entire weekend—just in case. She was juggling a briefcase, a laptop, and the leather and gold chain strap of a Chanel tote bag, which was sliding off her shoulder awkwardly as she moved quickly through the revolving door.

An orderly directed her to the fifth floor. The west wing of the modest city hospital had just been renovated, and the carpet still smelled new. It was a bright floral pattern that seemed ironic in such a place of death and decay. Even the fresh coat of paint could not cover up the obvious. Pain and fear permeated the stale air, replacing the usual hospital smells of antiseptic; the distinctive death-stench floated ever so prominently in the halls, where hope came to die.

This was a place where the dying went for treatment and respite in their final days. Nothing fancy about it. Just one big waiting room with plants, a few pictures of sailboats and sunsets; a place where patients' loved ones gathered and waited.

The wheels of her suitcase dragged skittishly on the rough surface. She stood in the center of the vast waiting area and scanned the room for Peter. She caught sight of him across a row of connected chairs that clashed badly with the bright colors of the carpeting.

Peter was seated, bent in half over a small satchel he was clutching atop his lap. He felt her presence before he even looked up as she walked toward him. His eyes were red and swollen. "It's happening," Peter said. "They're keeping him comfortable." He spoke as if he were speaking to a family member of a patient of his.

Hannah nodded. It was best to say nothing, for once.

The ward had twelve rooms and twenty-three beds. All but two rooms were occupied, and Anthony was in room number nine, a corner single adjacent to the staff's break room. The location had its advantages. Peter was able to raid the refrigerator after the second shift would leave, scoring pocketfuls of plain yogurt and pudding cups. It was the only two things that Anthony could keep down, usually. The ten-by-twelve space was all there was; that and a single window, which had been his world for nearly three time-suspended months.

There, Anthony lay fragile and pale, his bed facing east toward the open widow. An obstructed view of a half-city block across the street from a fast-food drive-through, a bus stop, and a chain-linked play lot were the only images Peter saw during his vigil.

That day, Anthony had been wearing a Miami Heat jersey—the one that Peter had given him after the team cinched the championship for the second time. It was right before he got really sick, even though he had been diagnosed in 2010. He was tall and strong and vibrant then, so filled with life and light. Just a regular guy, Peter would say, laughing with his buddies over a few Heinekens and some brats at Flanagan's after a game of hoops.

Hannah sat down next to Peter and let him reminisce. She would learn more about the man whom her husband loved. Together, they would sit and wait.

CHAPTER 58
★ ★ ★

ANTHONY BISHOP LOOKED LIKE AN ad from a
dating site touting the perfect match credentials—six
foot tall, honey-blond hair, cropped short on the sides and
moussed high in the front; thin, handsome features, soulful gray-blue eyes. He was a soft-spoken Aquarius with a
casual J. Crew style and a wide friendly smile. He drove a
bright yellow Jeep Explorer with ski racks on the hood.
He was charismatic, funny, kind, and extremely smart.
Always up for anything, he was a ball-buster sales executive
for an outdoor recreational retail chain who put people
into gear to climb mountains, drive hidden backroads, and
run marathons. Little did he know that at the prime of his
youth, he was about to face the challenge of his life. And
since Anthony was afraid of dying, it was nothing short of
a miracle that he found and fell in love with Peter, enabling
him to not have to face the journey alone.

To hear Anthony tell it, Peter was his reluctant prince. He
had noticed the handsome doctor who had come into the
club a second time where Anthony bartended on weekends to socialize and let off some steam from a full-throttle
workweek. But the two didn't speak to each other at first.

Peter was so shy that he later confessed that it took several months before he got the nerve to actually reach out to Anthony with a well-placed note left on his windshield. Within three weeks, they were trading emails and texts that led to a romantic and covert dinner in the city—and ultimately, to the hotel room adjacent and to a full-fledged love affair from that point moving forward.

Anthony shared a two-bedroom brick loft with a middle-aged divorced commodities broker who was a cross-dresser and amateur chef. It made for an interesting alter-lifestyle for Peter, for sure, but Anthony took it all in stride, knowing full well that Peter was married, and to Dr. Hannah Courtland-Murphy no less, which was more than intimidating.

One thing Anthony knew above all else—Peter loved him. Peter would often comment on how much he loved Anthony's little quirks; the fact that he could sing karaoke, cut hair, and was a Scrabble-Queen—a whiz with the tiles and crossword puzzles. He often bragged about how Anthony had even made the first round of *Jeopardy* once, back in '93. Together, they shared similar interests like hiking, biking, and roller-blading. They went clubbing, frequented the theater, and rescued a pair of Rottweilers named Betty and Ford. They loved to watch movies— the older the better, although they were often first in line to grab tickets to the latest sci-fi or summer blockbuster release.

Anthony never let on that he was lost without Peter when duties from home called him back to Ohio and his "first life." It was the saddest and yet most fulfilled that Anthony had ever felt, even being given only a fraction of Peter's time and devotion. Still, it did not matter. Anthony busied himself with his work and hobbies, knowing that the stolen weekdays and weekends proffered them were precious and not to be taken for granted. This, they both felt, made their relationship stronger and resilient when the time would come to face the biggest challenges of all.

Anthony's diagnosis in 2010 came as a shock, to say the least, to him and Peter. With no family support remaining in Anthony's inner circle due to his being disowned by his devout Protestant parents and relatives for coming out, all he had left was his lover, Peter.

"We'll get through this," Peter would assure him, knowing full well that the tests revealed a myriad of fatal complications resulting in him having had the HIV virus for years prior.

By 2010, Anthony was diagnosed with full-blown AIDS, as his immune system had begun to break down and was progressively unable to fend off infections. Complications followed for the next five years, ultimately rendering him weaker and sicker as time progressed. Gone were the days hiking at Blue Marsh Lake, cycling along Kelly Drive Loop taking in the river route and Boat House Row, or tossing around the Frisbee with Betty and Ford at the dog park. These, instead, were replaced with a regimen of antiretroviral drugs that Peter prescribed to help fight the virus in Anthony's body and an ongoing battery of tests on a monthly and weekly basis to monitor things called CD4 cells, and viral load. Daily concerns with anemia, blood sugar levels, and organ function became the norm. What didn't manage to weaken Anthony physically, did its work to render him broke with the limitations of health insurance causing him to have to eventually seek treatment through government-based programs.

The past several months had been an unspeakable torment, and Peter hated like hell to leave Anthony's side for even one minute, let alone to return home to his family and life in Ohio. He had never felt more helpless as a doctor and as a man. If ever there was any doubt of Peter's truth and sincerity about himself, it was made clear. He loved Anthony with all of his being.

He watched as Hannah slept on two chairs pushed together in an uncomfortable makeshift bed of deceit and lies, and yet—she was there. He didn't quite know if he revered her or hated her for stealing any precious minutes he might have had with Anthony as a strong, healthy man. Then Peter chastised himself for what he was thinking. He just wanted to go away—as far away as he could, to disappear and be alone. He wanted no responsibility at all. Nothing would matter without his heart. Hannah and the kids deserved more. It would not have been the first time that he had contemplated ending it all. Would that fix anything? Would it repair the lost time, the missing pieces of himself that now seemed lost forever?

He listened to the low monotone hum from the soda machine and counted the minutes as they ticked away.

He was living in a nightmare from which he could not awaken.

CHAPTER 59
★ ★ ★

THE NEXT MORNING, A TRACE of sunlight streamed in through the open window in Anthony's room, touching his pale cheek, setting his tired eyes alight with a flicker of hope; the same hope that gave him purpose to claim another day, again. Each precious one, with every slipping moment it contained afforded him another chance to see Peter once more . . . a little while longer, at best.

Peter had slept a few restless hours at Anthony's bedside, while Hannah slept in the waiting area, which was fine with her.

Peter had risen at five thirty to pee and to wash off in the utility sink just before the morning shift arrived on the ward. He journeyed the quiet corridor to the east end vending machine, where a handful of quarters and dimes brewed two cups of weak coffee; one for him and one for Hannah. A custodian with jingling keys got to work with his bucket and his mop, pushing around little puddles of suds on the floor in long, even strokes.

By the time Peter had returned to the room, Anthony was gone.

While Peter was not actually there sitting in the chair as he had done for eight straight weeks, it did not matter. His was the only face that Anthony saw right before he had closed his eyes.

Peter cried hard for several minutes, shaking in Hannah's arms. He felt strangely foreign to her—not like Peter at all, but like a man who had just had a good part of himself erased. He was a shell.

A container in which her husband once lived, but it was not *him* anymore. In a way, he had died unto her a long time ago—perhaps she just did not notice as poignantly as that very moment.

"What can I do?" Hannah's question was sincere.

God help her, she truly wanted to be there for him—in spite of everything. That's what she did. She helped people. Peter was in crisis, and it would be a long, long while before repair would be possible. There was no hope for their marriage undoubtedly, but there *was* hope that Peter could somehow rebuild his life again. It was not her place to say how or why. That would have to be up to him.

There was nothing more she could do. Just have him sign the papers she had brought that would give them both the freedom to move on. Hannah owed it to herself, her kids, and the people she helped daily to forge ahead. But for now, she would leave Peter to his own healing.

Hannah went back to her hotel room. The plan was that she would meet up with Peter later that evening for dinner. There, he would sign the papers, and then she would fly directly to New York first thing in the morning to meet with Global Network for the show signing. She was exhausted, both emotionally and physically, but she needed to remain strong. Soon the page would be turning on her new life.

CHAPTER 60
★ ★ ★

WEDNESDAY, AUGUST 19TH

ERIC STARED AT THE FISH tank across the room on
the bookshelf. An array of shiny, translucent fish swam
manically from side to side. The air pump gurgled hyp-
notically, and the aquarium glowed, illuminating the walls
with a peaceful cast of light. Several large posters and concert paraphernalia loomed in glossy tribute to his favorite
band, Code X, on the four walls littered with more photos
ripped from a yearbook—and candid stills of a teenage
girl smiling from the center of a high school cheerleading
squad. Around her face was drawn a heart with permanent
marker, and written above, the pronouncement: ERIC &
MELISSA FOREVER!

He stared at the ceiling, listening to the droning hum
of the fish tank, and laid out his plan carefully. School had
only been back in session for two weeks.

Getting into Principal Steller's e-mail was easy, Coach
Rainer's roster was a cinch, and breaking the code into
administration's database was a walk in the park, as Eric
had possessed the key to his father's confidential file cabi-

net since he was ten, in which all of the faculty passwords were logged. Being the son of the school district Superintendent had its advantages, but it did not change the fact that Grant Leary, the insolent linebacker whose photo was speared through the eye with a pocketknife on the corkboard hung over his bed, had to die. And if it meant taking out half the school with him, then so be it.

CHAPTER 61
★ ★ ★

GRANT LEARY WAS A GEEK-FACED all-star jock-monkey with perfect teeth and privileges directly linked to his Neanderthal talent for moving the ball when it mattered most. But mysteriously shrinking attendance records, and erratic and excessive tardiness showed a different view of the ace superstar. A regretful and steadily plunging GPA over the past many months now caused his junior-year transcripts to read like a tragic trilogy, as his hopes for scoring a paid scholarship to Carolina State plummeted like a bad stock.

All without so much as a flinch of hesitation, Eric worked his plan with exact precision, bringing down the six-foot-four star linebacker with several well-placed keystrokes and the click of a mouse.

But that was only step one of his plan. Leary was a member of The Church of Jesus Christ of Latter-day Saints and fancied Melissa Gates for his wife—*one* of his wives, no doubt—lusting for her as did most every other red-blooded guy in school. Eric seethed. *He would never have her! Never!*

Rumor in the halls had the two slated as sure bets for

King & Queen of Harrisburg High School's junior prom. Such ceremonious unions only led to no good, as far as Eric was concerned. He would have to stop it from happening—at any and all costs.

For the sole purpose of incriminating the meathead jock, Eric sent an encoded email to Principal Steller, under the guise of being a concerned student. Eric downloaded all of his own letters and poems, along with an anonymous tip warning Steller of the "troubled" student, Grant Leary's, threatening alter-ego behavior toward the school, further claiming that Leary was plotting to strike in retaliation against the administration for "botching" up his records.

Eric typed the warning in boldface letters across the screen, I WOULD NOT PUT ANYTHING PAST THIS LUNITIC . . . HE IS A THREAT TO OUR STUDENTS AND FACULTY!

In a flash, he sent the damaging lies across the Internet to Steller's desktop. But, unbeknownst to him, the slanderous fated message had also been copied to *Hannah's* computer—sent with a batch of attachments previously forwarded to *her* at the radio station. All of the attached files forwarded both to Principal Steller as well as to the radio station now appeared on Jon Novotny's screen as he was perusing Hannah's messages one last time before the end of the day, as was his usual practice.

The files were all meticulously altered to be untraceable—with the exception of one—the one that Eric overlooked in haste—still tagged with his full name printed next to his bogus email address: Eric Johansson.

A quick succession of clicks and Jon was able to locate the I.P. address from the errant email leading to the culprit's location somewhere in Harrisburg, PA.

"Gottcha! You little bastard!" Jon exclaimed when he realized what had happened, nearly knocking over his coffee in the process.

CHAPTER 62
★ ★ ★

T
HE PHONE IN HANNAH'S HOTEL room rang unanswered on the bedside nightstand. Jon Novotny fidgeted on the other end of the line with nervous energy. For some reason, her cellphone was gong straight to voice mail. "C'mon, Hannah. *Be there . . . be there.*"

No answer. Hannah was immersed in the soothing torrent of powerful shower jets, pounding away the tension of too many months measure. Her dead-as-a-doorknob iPhone had not been charged in too many hours sitting at the hospital with no cell service. She had not thought to recharge it in the wake of the events in the past twelve hours.

There was still no answer twenty minutes later, when Jon tried her hotel room, yet again.

Hannah finally emerged from the shower. A no-nonsense type, she gave her face a quick dusting of translucent powder, dabbed on some lip gloss, and a swipe of blush. She slipped into a pair of comfortable jeans, donned a cotton blouse, slipped into leopard print pumps, and gave herself a finishing spritz of Channel No. 5. In ten minutes flat she was out the door—her still-dead cell phone in her purse.

Hannah met Peter in the hotel restaurant for convenience and ease. They both needed a good meal, but Peter was loath to eat much of it, understandably. They had planned a swift, public goodbye that would be sealed with the signing of the divorce documents, a few more unavoidable tears, and the mutual promise to maintain utmost respect for each other and unwavering love and continued commitment for the well-being of their children and grandchildren.

Peter agreed to attend therapy sessions with a colleague at Hannah's insistence, as was outlined in the divorce decree. She knew that he would need it. She would have sole custody of Olivia, who was still in high school, and he, responsibility for her college tuition and fees.

Hannah's determination to bring closure to everything was only further fueled by the confusion and bitterness she felt by Peter's deep sorrow and distraction over losing Anthony, his lover of over ten years, compared to the cogency of their marriage of thirty-eight years—a contrast that utterly consumed her at the very moment. It was evident that this final step was well overdue. The time had come for Hannah, and for Peter, to start their new lives . . . to move on.

Hannah returned well after eleven to the hotel room to find the message light on the desk phone flashing. She puzzled and then reached for her smartphone. It was dead, and she chastised herself for not having noticed. She had been unreachable for how long? Quickly, she found the cord and plugged it into the wall and then to the phone. She checked her messages to see if Olivia had been trying to reach her. Thankfully, she had not, but there were dozens of text messages from Jon Novotny. She dialed the front desk, kicking off her shoes and settling onto the bed.

"This is Dr. Hannah Courtland-Murphy. I believe I have a message?"

"Yes, Dr. Hannah—a Jon Novotny has been trying to reach you. Please, contact him right away. He says it's urgent."

She contemplated the time. Eleven thirty-eight. Couldn't it wait? What on earth was it now? Her work followed her everywhere! It was more than she could take sometimes. Considering her important meeting in the morning, she feared that maybe there had been a change in plans with Global Network, so she scrolled through her contact list for Jon's cell number.

"*Hannah—?*"

"Whoa, Jon. Is everything okay?"

"It's psycho-boy—he emailed you. Only it wasn't exactly intended for *you*. He copied us inadvertently on a transmission to a Principal Steller."

"Yeah, so . . . ?"

"This has got to be a *kid!* His name is Eric Johansson. He's a student."

"I knew it!" Hannah stood straight up. Her instincts were rarely wrong. "Did you track down where he lives? What school?"

"I pulled a few strings in research, and they tracked the principal's email address, and you're not going to believe this—he's close, Hannah. He's in Harrisburg, Pennsylvania. But it's his personal email address and home phone number. No idea what school."

"That's about a hundred miles from here," Hannah calculated. All the while she was talking to Jon, she was fumbling with the electrical cord from her laptop, which was also dead. Finally, she successfully plugged it into the wall outlet and booted up. She positioned the screen in the dim light on top of the bed. Manipulating the tiny mouse tracker, she navigated her way into her email files and opened the document.

"I think I see it. There! I got it . . . it says it's from a *Grant Leary*?"

Jon explained, "Look at the return address. It's from our wonder-boy, all right. He forwarded all the others under the alias, Grant Leary. His real name is Eric Johansson."

She scanned the message. The threatening words sent prickly chills right through her.

"He says he's going to *waste the enemy in fiery flames . . . all Dragons die by my might . . .*. Why on earth would he be pretending to be this guy Grant Leary? I don't get it. Good call, Jon. Whatever this means, I'm sure the principal would love to know about it."

Jon paused. He knew that he had already impressed her with his savvy detective work, but why stop there?

"Want me to send this Stellar an email? Give him the heads-up on this thing?"

"No—no need to that. I think I'll take it from here." She sighed. "I'll reach out to him in the morning on my way to the airport and forward the rest of the email documents to him, so the school counselors handle things from there. I'm sure it's just an elaborate prank. A rivalry between two students or something. Forward me Steller's home phone number and email address, will you?"

"I'll do it right away . . ."

"Great job—really. You are quite the detective!"

"No problem, Doc. It's all in a day's work. And hey, best of luck tomorrow at the signing."

"Thanks, Jon. Goodnight."

Sleepily, she climbed into bed and perused the file containing the messages that Eric had sent her over the last several months, including the most recent ones he had forwarded under the name "Grant Leary." She frowned when she re-read the trail of bitter angst and threatening promises of doom. *What was this guy capable of?* she wondered.

Here was an obviously brilliant but disillusioned young man. *But why?* Why was he doing all this? And why did he choose *her* to turn to, yet never give himself an outlet for her to help? Perhaps, she reasoned, this twist of fate was a way that she could, after all, help Eric. Notifying the principal was the least she could do for him. He was obviously crying out for help.

She drifted asleep and dreamt of herself being caught in a labyrinth of school hallways. There were hospital beds engulfed in flames and people screaming and running in all directions. She felt herself running blindly in the heat, exhausted, confused, and frightened. Off in the distance, she could see Peter . . . fading farther and farther from view in the thick, wafting smoke. School bells and sirens rang, louder and louder, drowning out her voice as she called out to him—"*Peter!*"

In an instant, he was gone. And the giant dragons were upon her.

CHAPTER 63
★ ★ ★

"NO!" SHE BOLTED STRAIGHT UP in bed, panting. A cold sweat sprang from her forehead as she sat, shivering in the darkness, disoriented and wet with perspiration. The alarm clock on the desk loomed five a.m. and was blaring. The nightmare, which quickly slipped into the half-light, was one hell of a wake-up call, she thought, turning off the alarm.

She steadied herself and slid from the covers. Parting the heavy hotel drapes, she looked out the window. It was gray and overcast. Hopefully, she would make it out of Philadelphia before it stormed. The news had been predicting more rain all week across the coast. Autumn was coming fast.

She shook the disturbing dream from her consciousness. She had to. It was, among other things, the first official day of the rest of her life as an unmarried woman now, with Peter's signature having sealed the deal. That would take some getting used to. And secondly, it was also the day of her signing with Global Network. It truly was a day of "firsts." She had to pull herself together fast and shift gears for the morning ahead. Her flight was at eight o'clock.

Marney would positively crucify her if she was late for the most important deal of her life.

Heavily, she moved across the room, clicked on the morning news, and then headed for the bathroom for an invigorating shower. Steam and soap would do their magic.

She turned on the water jets, adjusted the temperature just right, and stepped into the full force of the pulsating water jets.

In less than an hour, Hannah would be on her way to New York. It would be a short flight to La Guardia, where Marney would be waiting for her with a car. She chose to wear the navy blue Prada pantsuit and sensible Italian pumps with matching Chanel scarf because it always made her feel powerful and confident to coordinate from head to toe, and any shade of blue was an asset to her light complexion and honey-blond hair. She removed her wedding band from her left hand to her right ring finger and added a gold bangle to her wrist. A flat gold crucifix on a thin chain gleamed against her neck. She was ready.

Outside, the skies were menacing, but she checked in with the airport and all flights were on time. She hung up with United Airlines and then phoned the number that Jon had given her the night before for the principal. She had a few minutes before her Uber car would arrive.

A young woman answered.

"Yes—Principal Stellar, please," Hannah said into her now fully charged phone.

"I'm sorry, ma'am. Mr. Stellar is out of town. He is expected back on Monday. Would you care to leave a message?"

Hannah shouldered her carry-on bag. "No. Tell me, though, can Mr. Stellar retrieve his email from where he is?"

"No, I'm afraid not," the woman replied. "He's camping

in Quarryville with his family. I'm the pet sitter. He's asked to have all of his calls sent to text or voice mail. He'll check them when he gets cell service."

Hannah paused, then asked. "Would you happen to know which school Mr. Steller works at?"

The woman hedged. "No, I'm sorry. I do think it's a high school, though. Just not sure which one."

"Thank you," Hannah said. "I'm sure it can wait until he returns. No message." Then she hung up.

Stellar never got the email messages in the first place, Hannah deduced. The phony "Grant Leary" transmissions were still stored in his queue!

She thought in a fleeting moment of instinct and wished that she could have connected with someone at the school who was connected to Eric Johansson, just as the app sounded with the arrival of her car. It was time to go.

She shook her head. Enough of this kid and his shenanigans! She had to catch her flight. She would make a note to call Stellar on Monday and pass on the whole ordeal to the people it concerned.

Grabbing her laptop and briefcase, she headed out the door, leaving the television, which had been muted, still on with its images of the macabre drama in Harrisburg from the night before continuing to unfold in horrifying and vivid detail.

Hannah tried phoning the radio station from the terminal. A weak signal prevented connection on the other end of her cell phone until she got to the gate, where she sent Olivia a quick text asking her to wish her luck with the signing, along with a few heart emojis and the Woman Scientist emoji, which always made Olivia smile. She would be just heading to her first class of the day, AP Biology. Olivia was her little genius in the making, and she always gave her daughter all the support she could, even though, academically, she didn't need it.

Hannah then started to dial Jon at the radio station, but remembered that they were all in the morning staff meeting for another half hour. She figured that she would call him once she had arrived at La Guardia.

The airline attendant called for early boarding. Traveling first-class had the decisive disadvantage of being on display as a cabin full of gaping passengers filed by on their way to business coach. She would wait. Once on board, she would order a mimosa to calm her nerves.

She stayed seated in the terminal, flipped open her laptop, and clicked onto her email. Her pulse quickened as she read the subject line—it was a new message from Eric Johansson. And this time, he was finally responding to her directly!

She stared in disbelief at the subject line and finally clicked on it to open the contents. Time stood still as the venomous words burned on the screen: BITCH—HELP *ME*? WHEN DRAGONS DIE! HOW ABOUT TODAY? KA-BOOM!!! KEEP WATCHING . . .

What in the world did he mean by keep watching? What was he trying to tell her?

She waited as the passengers for her flight filed onto the jetway—mostly businessmen in suits. Then, a jarring hush came over the terminal as all eyes became riveted to the suspended television screens all around.

Hannah puzzled, then gasped when she felt a hand clamp down on her shoulder, nearly causing her to jump out of her skin as she stood up.

"*Hannah! It's me!*"

She shot around to find Jon standing behind her with a backpack slung on his shoulder. He was panting, half-winded, having just run from his arrival gate clear across the terminal. He was breathing so hard he was bent in two.

"What on earth? Jon . . . what are you doing here?"

"I just flew in—obviously you have seen the news, right?" he said, gesturing to the television monitors pulsating with the continuing breaking story, which was scrolling across the bottom of the screen.

The bloody massacre, which occurred at a residence overnight, was caused by a suspected homemade bomb that had been detonated in the basement, killing a family of five. The reporter went on, "Authorities have been on the scene since daybreak, just now beginning the removal of the charred bodies from the cindered rubble . . . "

"There . . . there's been an explosion," he panted. "It's all over the networks." He checked her face. "Jesus, are you just seeing this now? A bomb went off in a house last night in Harrisburg. Everyone inside sleeping was killed. Hannah—it was *Grant Leary's* family."

"Oh my God!" Hannah's legs collapsed, giving out beneath her. Jon grabbed her arm just before she fell. "I didn't know." Then, she paled. "Jon, what if—?"

"That's exactly what I am thinking. Didn't sleep all night. I caught a red-eye here, figuring . . . "

"Oh my God! Eric Johansson emailed me not twenty minutes ago," Hannah breathed, closing her laptop and gathering up her things. "He had a warning. He told me that he hasn't even gotten *started* yet! You don't *think* . . . ?"

Jon waited exactly five seconds for Hannah to answer her own question, pulling out his phone to order up a car.

Then, it took her less time than that to determine that she was not getting onto the plane to New York.

Instead, she turned to Jon and said, "*Let's go!*"

CHAPTER 64
★ ★ ★

HANNAH AND JON RUSHED TO the rental car counter, where Jon finalized the rental and Hannah took advantage of the Wi-Fi signal while there still was one. She did a quick search for dragon mascots for high schools in the Dauphin County area, which was Principal Steller's area code. She took a random shot. The results brought her three possibilities. She chose the third one and clicked onto the link. Oddly, it took several tries to get through to the website. The system was jammed.

"C'mon, . . . C'mon . . . TALK to me!" she pleaded as precious seconds ticked away.

A moment later, the images appeared in animated block letters, which seemed almost surreal as they gleamed on the screen, "WELCOME TO HARRISBURG HIGH SCHOOL." A revolving cartoon dragon caught her eye in the upper right-hand corner. She clicked on it and noticed that the dragon icon had cyber connected to the physical education site for the school called Coach's Corner. She quickly learned that the Dragons were the school's football team. They were champions three years running, headed by Coach Rainer, third-string former runningback for Penn State. A calendar of upcoming events was posted, touting an all-school pep rally scheduled for ten o'clock that very morning in the student assembly hall, named *Bremen's Hall*.

Hannah's stomach tightened. She recognized the reference from EJ's rantings. It was what they meant by "gut instinct," and hers was firing off. She clicked down further and immediately found what she feared—the team's linebacker, Grant Leary's, name was at the top and center of the team roster. He was a handsome boy with a tussle of wavy brown hair and a broad, earnest grin. Next to him was a pixie-faced cheerleader named Melissa Gates. The caption beneath their images read: "Your 2015 Homecoming King and Queen? Click here to vote!"

Melissa . . . sweet Melissa . . . letter number nine! Eric's words burned in the file folder shoved in her carry-on bag next to her now-crumpled Prada blazer. It was clear that something awful was still going to happen. It was in motion.

There was nothing she could do, or was there?

Jon pulled up in a Subaru Crosstrek SUV, and she climbed in. "I'll fill you in on the way," she said, tossing the bags into the back. She then punched in the coordinates for Harrisburg High School on the console with trembling fingers as Jon peeled out of the parking lot, heading south on I-95. They were both praying that God's grace, and sheer luck, would get them there—hopefully, in time.

CHAPTER 65

★ ★ ★

WHEN THEY HAD REACHED SEVENTY-FIVE miles per hour, Hannah fumbled for her cell and began dialing 9-1-1 with trembling hands. Instantly, she was connected to the county police.

The voice on the other end of the phone asked her to hold.

"*Hold!* They put me on goddamn hold! Drive faster!" Hannah ordered. Jon was already breaking all the rules, but he floored it. They sped faster toward Veterans Memorial Highway toward Exit 7.

An eternity passed, and then a supervisor came on the line.

"Ma'am, I'm Officer Nolan . . . can I have your name, please?"

"Yes, sir, I'm Dr. Hannah Courtland-Murphy of Venture Media's syndicate talk show *Straight Talk with Dr. Hannah*. I think I might have information linked to the Leary bombing. Listen to me—I have reason to believe that Harrisburg High School in Dauphin County may be a target. You have got to call for a lock down! A student may be planning a rampage. In fact, I'm sure of it!"

"Where are you now, Ms. Murphy?"

She strained to think, glancing at her watch. It was nine thirty-five. The rally was set to begin at ten o'clock.

"Did you hear me, Officer? I'm telling you that you've GOT to get those kids out of there! There is a rally happening in Bremen's Hall. You have to act NOW!"

"One moment, please . . ."

"Son-of-a-*bitch!*" They were no doubt attempting to trace the call. Hannah slammed her fist on the dashboard. A throbbing migraine was pounding at her temples. She feared the worst. Why should they believe her? What proof was there that she even *was* who she said she was in the first place? They could have been talking to some crackpot for all they knew! Still, shouldn't they take every call seriously, regardless?

Road signs whizzed by, indicating that they were just miles from the I-76 merge toward Valley Forge, which would be another eighty-four long miles to Harrisburg. Jon floored it, barreling through the gray haze.

CHAPTER 66
★ ★ ★

ERIC WATCHED THE DOORS INTENTLY from the curb. Waiting. A momentary glimpse passed before his eyes of a vacation that he and his parents once took in Wyoming. There was the amusement park in Houston another time . . . his mother cutting vegetables on the kitchen counter . . . the skateboard he got for Christmas in two thousand seven; his computer games, the dog they had when they lived on Jenner Street with one blue eye and one brown; the dentist and his cold steel drill, the first day of high school. Then, he thought of Melissa; of cutting his lip two summers ago on the handlebars of his mountain bike, trying to impress her; Grant Leary and other boys, ogling her from the sidelines when she cheered. The times that she might have once tossed him a glance in passing in the hall. Had she smiled? He could not remember. Did she laugh when all the others iced him out and pointed and laughed under their breath, calling him a freak and a waste of humanity? They were just images—quick flashes—and then they were gone.

He hadn't given most of it much thought in the recent past, and yet, there had been one thing that he could not stop thinking about for months. It was always there—a way out. He was ready. As ready as he would ever be. The emails had been sent and the fates had been sealed. Just in case, he had printed off a copy of the last one sent to that hack, Dr. Hannah, and jammed it into his jeans pocket.

There was only one last thing to do. He crossed himself quickly. In all actuality, he didn't believe that God gave a rat's ass about him, but in such instances, one could never be sure about anything. He figured he would call on Christ for the forgiveness promised, even though he hated fucking Jews.

CHAPTER 67

★ ★ ★

HARRISBURG, PA

OWEN BRADY SLAMMED THE METAL locker—the last one on the far left, bottom row, with the busted lock that only worked when you jiggled it. A colorful array of lollipops were still taped to the front door; remnants of his initiation one week prior. He fastened the last button on his police-issued blues. His hair was still wet from the shower, but it was worth it for the extra twenty-five reps on the kettle bells in the gym that morning. He had slicked the cowlick back with some gel, which would get his balls busted from the other guys, but he didn't care. He had other problems, namely, that he had just moved back in with his middle-aged mother due to a split between him and his ex-fiancé that started in Cancun two months back and was still holding strong. The new job coming through was a Godsend, but it wouldn't be easy to consider himself as being a *real* cop until he had earned his stripes so to speak and saved up enough for his own place. At twenty-three, he wasn't necessarily waiting for his ship to come in—a skiff that could hold water would do.

He tied the rigid shoelaces and thought about an argument he had with his mother just that morning. "You don't have to do my laundry, Mom. I can take care of that myself," he had said as he gave her a swift kiss on the cheek, his army green gym bag in hand as he headed off to the station.

"What? I have been doing somebody's laundry for the past thirty years, so why should now be any different?"

He hated that she felt the need to baby him. Hadn't he gotten enough of that treatment with the initiation? *Geeze!* He didn't know what was worse, living back home, or being the newest rookie on the force getting razed at every turn. He would need to win respect on all levels before those who mattered would call him *Officer*. It was all that mattered.

He grabbed his gear and headed out to the lot. He hated the way that his gun leather creaked every time he made a move. It was newly issued and hadn't been fully broken in yet. Today, he would be riding shotgun with Ostrowski, an experienced veteran of thirty-five years with the Dauphin County PD. *Damn!* he thought. *This one hates to do any paperwork—thinks that's what I'm here for. Paper training as he calls it."*

Ostrowski slid his middle-aged gut beneath the steering wheel, called in that they were "10-8," in service and ready for duty. He then chided, "Okay, 'boot,' let's see what the day brings."

Brady was calm-faced and obedient. This was no time to fend off insults.

They barely made it out onto the main road when a car with faulty taillights caught Ostrowski's eagle eye. He pulled the vehicle over and approached the car cautiously. "Stay here," he said, grabbing his ticket book. The dash cam recorded the exchange. He delivered a stern warning to the driver, a harried office worker gushing with apologies. After a few minutes of friendly exchange, he let her go.

Yep, Brady yawned. *It was going to be a slow day.*

Two traffic crash calls later, a potential break-in inquiry, and a flat tire assist rounded out the morning with little effect.

"Come on," Ostrowski said, sensing Brady's dip in energy. "Let me show you something they don't teach you in field training—where to score the best coffee in town."

CHAPTER 68
★ ★ ★

A T PRECISELY TEN A.M., ERIC Johansson walked through the double doors, past the reception office, and made his way down the long, empty corridor to the doorway of the assembly hall. Remarkably, he went unnoticed. The school receptionist had been away from her station just long enough for him to slip by.

The rally was just getting started, and the crowd of students was buzzing with excitement. He could imagine Melissa, dressed in her cheerleading outfit, pumping her fists in the air to rev up the bleachers in a flurry of hoots and whistles. The band started up, and pandemonium swelled from behind the massive wooden doors. Through the sliver of glass, he could see the members of the Dragons football team, jogging out onto the floor—minus one Grant Leary. *Had the authorities released the names yet from his handiwork earlier that morning?* It appeared not.

He took a deep breath, shut off his mind, and pulled the Kel-Tec .223 semi-automatic rifle from the duffel bag that swung low on his shoulder, letting the bag fall to the floor. He located the charging handle, shoved the cartridge into the magazine well, and locked it into place with a click. His finger trembled as he placed it on the trigger and pushed open the door with his open palm. He paused, took a deep breath, and immediately began shooting rounds from left to right in a sweeping motion, moving forward into the assembly hall, shouting at the top of his lungs, "Die! Bastards, die!" Manic and methodical, he watched without affect as the bodies dropped in his wake.

First down was the stunned security guard, Freddie, who, only for a second, might have recognized the boy and pleaded for his life with a quivering, pathetic gesture just seconds before Eric filled his chest with a spray of bullets.

And for thirteen eternal minutes more he moved his way across the massive room, starting with the chaotic scene of students jumping from the bleachers, picking off freshmen and jocks, geeks and honor students; children of mothers and fathers, sisters and brothers. The holy and the haunted—teachers, coaches, and counselors—anyone in his path.

Brady and Ostrowski had pulled up to a coffee shop on Green Street and were nursing two steaming cups of joe on a sticky park bench and having a heart-to-heart about wearing the badge.

"I hear you did time," Ostrowski said, removing the lid and blowing into the paper cup.

"Yes, sir. Two tours in Iraq. Twelve months each, back to back. Mostly serviced gun trucks for convoy security, but I did do some grunt work in the red zone on my second deploy."

"What was that like?" Ostrowski asked, partly to make conversation and partly because he wanted to know, seeing as how he had missed the draft in '71 due to a viral infection that had laid him up for months.

"It was a bag of dicks most of the time, but you get

through it. Not much different than working the grind out here some days, I suppose," Brady opined.

"Well, all I can say is that you shouldn't let the weight of all this unnerve you. Don't believe what they say about throwing out what you learned in the academy—that none of it is real. It's not true. No matter what happens, never lie about a screw-up. If you lie, you're out. Embrace and own your mistakes." He flicked a gnat off his cuff with a beefy thumb.

"Yeah, some situations can be rough, I guess," Brady said, wondering if he had the stuff to make a good cop.

The surly cop chuckled, raising a freckled index finger. "I doubt this is any different from what it was you went through. Remember, losing your focus is the number one thing that'll get you killed—or worse, lead to more problems," he said, proving that even crusty old cops had a sense of humor.

"I'll try to remember that, sir."

"You don't have to call—"

Just then, their radios squawked. *"Multiple shots reported in the vicinity of Harrisburg High School. Possible active shooter."*

"That's a block away," Ostrowski said, reaching for his radio. He delivered a series of codes rapid-fire into his radio and then barked the command, "Dump the bean juice. Let's roll!"

Brady ditched the half-drunk coffee cups into the dumpster and jumped into the car. They peeled away with the siren blaring and lights blazing toward Market Street.

CHAPTER 69

★ ★ ★

BETTY BRADY CAUGHT THE NEWS bulletin just as she was about to press her son's police-issued shirt with a perfect crease down the sleeve that was her specialty. A female news anchor with a pretty face delivered the update about the events unfolding at the high school standing in a half-empty parking lot blocks away from the school. "Word has it, according to eyewitnesses, that at least one gunman opened fire on the students at an assembly in the school's Bremen's Hall."

Betty gasped and set the steam iron on its stand and looked up to watch the television screen in the living room. Her heart quickened as she heard the anchorwoman report that every police officer in the county was descending upon the tragic scene, in addition to federal SWAT teams, who had begun swarming the area.

She grabbed her cellphone from the credenza and scrolled for Owen's name. "Pick up . . . pick up," she said, her stomach tightening with nerves. *Surely he would be okay.* It was only his first week on the job.

Brady and Ostrowski pulled up first on the scene, stopping short of the main entrance. Throwing open the car doors, they pulled their weapons and crouched down, for cover, waiting for backup. Brady tossed his unanswered phone onto the floorboard, where it continued to buzz. The sound of shots being fired reverberated in the direction of the assembly hall. They were coming from an automatic weapon.

"I'm going in!" Ostrowski said, tugging on his vest and feeling for his radio to inform dispatch. "You stay—"

Just then, as he tried to stand, he teetered unsteadily and fell backward to the ground, clutching his left arm.

"Sir—are you hit, sir?" Brady called out, moving around to the back end of the police car to see. Ostrowski was writhing in pain and could barely breathe. An ambulance skidded up, and Brady motioned for help. "Something's wrong. I think he's having a heart attack!" Brady said, backing away to allow the medics to assess the situation.

The perimeter was filling up with police cars and medical support from every angle. A huge black truck rolled onto the campus sidewalk, and heavily geared men climbed out of the back to swarm the north end, where the classrooms were located. A news chopper hovered overhead.

The shots ceased momentarily, and then started up again—a quick succession of staccato blasts echoing across the campus.

Brady ducked through a stream of first responders in the opposite direction—eastward toward the assembly hall from which he and Ostrowski had heard the first shots.

Brady ran around to the back end of the gymnasium and slipped into the service entrance off the locker rooms. He was in.

From this vantage point he could hear the screaming and commotion emanating from the gymnasium. Several frantic students rushed past him in tears, wailing and frightened. One girl grabbed his arm and wouldn't let go. He pried her off and motioned for them to run out. "Hands over your heads—go! Go!"

Then, he crept around to the access door to the gym and could see the shooter firing. His back was to Brady. He had stopped momentarily, perhaps to reload, as students scattered in all directions, ducking and taking cover any way they could.

Then, it got eerily quiet. Students were hiding beneath the bleachers, stuck between the shooter and any viable exit.

Brady held steady. He had been here before. It was northern Iraq all over, only without the dust and heat. *He was once again on the back of an Army truck, watching as the women and children scattered like ants as enemy gunfire rained on them from the tree line.* It was no different.

When the shooter heard Brady's radio squawk, he spun around and faced him dead-on. Brady lifted the revolver and lined up his mark. He did not wait a beat, or for Eric to discover that his clip was indeed empty just before he squeezed the trigger. Brady fired—felling the boy in one clean shot.

In seconds, the first responders and SWAT team rushed into the assembly hall. And an army of soldiers were upon him.

CHAPTER 70
★ ★ ★

HANNAH AND JON ARRIVED AT the school to a horrendous scene. There were roadblocks in every direction. Swat teams and bomb squads were everywhere, along with a militia of police cars, fire, and rescue trucks. Several police helicopters hovered above as a stream of frightened teenagers filed outside of the building in a straight line, with their hands over their heads; some silent, others wailing. Jon and Hannah came to a complete stop at a blockade.

By the time they received clearance to proceed on through, the news teams had begun to arrive, uncoiling their cables and positioning their camera lights trained on the tiny brick school. Somehow, it looked small and vulnerable in the center of all the chaos and confusion surrounding it.

"Go around over there!" Hannah directed as Jon slowed the SUV past a swell of onlookers, who were standing on the curb. They inched their way slowly through the line of photographers and bystanders as the crowd miraculously parted to let them through as shouts of recognition caused a commotion all its own. *Look! Hey, Dr. Hannah! It's her!*

It was one time in her career that she wished that she was someone else.

The first bomb, a crude homemade explosive made of steel pipe and hobby shop fuses, detonated in Grant Leary's basement early that morning, killing him, his parents, two sisters, and their cocker spaniel, who were all sleeping upstairs. Grant awoke to flames shooting through the floor beneath his bed and was helpless to assist the girls, whose muffled screams he could hear in the darkness as they were quickly consumed by the merciless smoke.

The second bomb was found after the evacuation. It had been planted in a gym locker at the school and was programmed to go off nearly six hours later—precisely at ten forty a.m., just after Eric would have finished his work—and left this world. Miraculously, it failed. It was intended to rip the roof off of the school and finish off the rest of the student body and faculty.

Thankfully, Hannah's tip to Sergeant Nolan prompted an all-out siege, as undercover agents and local officers descended on the school just as Eric began his rampage, but far from in time to save his victims.

Eric Johansson was swiftly felled by an officer's well-aimed bullet to the chest at close range, but not before twenty-one students, staff, and faculty were tragically slaughtered in the bloodbath. This, along with Grant Leary and his entire family, brought the total death count toll to twenty-nine souls. The cheerleader, Melissa Gates was badly wounded, but survived.

Following the siege, authorities combed the grounds for additional explosives or arsenal. Their investigation retrieved two small handguns and a hand grenade in Eric Johansson's locker. He had lived only four miles from the school.

When the authorities arrived at his parents' house, a search found additional weaponry and a "dummy bomb" used to fashion the explosive used in the Leary massacre.

Eric's computer had been left on, and a framed photograph of a cheerleader was smashed to pieces. A suicide note matching the one found on his body was typed on the screen in the form of a Word document. It was addressed to Dr. Hannah Courtland-Murphy, the syndicated radio talk show psychologist.

Words, she knew, that would forever haunt her, were blurred nearly illegible on the blood-soaked note found in Eric's jean pocket: YOU BLEW IT, DOC. SO DID I . . . REMEMBER MY NAME!

No, she would never forget.

The Johanssons were stunned and paralyzed with grief. By evening, they were not talking to anyone, except the high-profile lawyer who saw the story reported on the morning news and had instructed them not to speak. Hannah, who avoided the press and police, sat with them and prayed with them. She shared the trail of emails that he had sent her; the cryptic clues that led her there. They wept in each other's arms, disbelieving every second of the surreal events unfolding. Wayne Johansson knew that he would need to reconcile what he knew about his family history with his wife. On some level, he was left feeling that he singularly had let Eric down; a regret he would struggle the rest of his days to accept. One which he shared with the good Dr. Hannah behind closed doors at a non-disclosed location.

Hannah would miss the signing meeting with Global Network, having agreed to stay on to offer grief counseling in any way that she could. There would be plenty of time later to answer the barrage of questions from the chief of police and later, the district attorney. The media would continue to be relentless, but would have to wait.

Jon had managed to connect with Marney, who would arrange for her to conduct the signing meeting with

Friedman and his cohorts via a conference call connection later that morning. Hannah's lawyer, Patrick Cavanaugh, had power of attorney, and would be sitting in her place. Everyone had agreed that, under the circumstances, the station would postpone her ceremonially adding her own signature to the contract on a separate occasion.

"I'll be staying on to counsel the kids who will want to talk to someone about what went on here," she later told Friedman's people collectedly on the call from her room at the Howard Johnson's hotel near the school. "I will be staying on here for as long as they need me."

Then, she hung up the phone and broke down in a torrent of silent and gasping sobs that had been years coming—an inexorable display of grief that racked her body until she could barely breathe.

She sat on the weathered carpet, slumped and exhausted against the wall, as the sirens, carrying the injured and newly minted souls, wailed in the distance.

Brady found his phone that had been rolling on the floorboard as he drove the car back to the police lot. There were fifteen messages from his mom. He decided that he would knock off a few minutes early and head to the hospital to check on Ostrowski, and then head home. He would quickly call her back to say he was all right.

When he walked in the door, his sergeant and a cadre of staff and other officers were there to greet him with a standing ovation. He was stunned. It was surreal and unnerving at the same time.

Several reporters were waiting to talk to him. "Officer Brady—a word. What was it like to stare down the shooter?"

"Is it true that you are a rookie with the force?"

"How are you feeling?"

Brady dodged the flashbulbs and questions as he made his way to his Mustang Cobra. "I did my job, that's all," he said matter-of-factly.

He just wanted to go home and have a beer.

CHAPTER 71

★ ★ ★

GLOBAL STUDIOS
NEW YORK CITY

MARNEY PACED AROUND THE SMALL coffee table in the waiting area outside of the glass conference room quickly filling with people—important people. She looked nervous and peaked after a tough interrogation from the homeland security authorities. It was clear that she had no knowledge of Eric Johansson, or the emails sent to Hannah. In fact, she was shaken and sickened by the news flooding the cable and local networks about the bombing and shooting in Harrisburg that clearly were the actions of a deranged young man. She continued to text Jon Novotny for updates.

Hannah's lawyer had just arrived, and the time was drawing near. *Everything was riding on today . . . everything.* She checked once again with a staff assistant to confirm that a conference phone would be in the room to patch-in Hannah's call.

Everything was ready.

The elevator doors sprang open, and Bumpy Friedman

and his designer-suited team emerged. He paused, and then approached Marney with an outstretched hand and a wide grin. Needless to say, the network was impressed with Hannah's altruism and professional dedication. Bumpy himself was later quoted in the *Times* as saying, "Hell— our number one host is out saving the world, performing miracles of humanitarian and heroic valor. We'll definitely hold her seat on the co-anchor's couch here at *The Gab* . . . for when her wings cool down. She is precisely the healing and light that we want—a modern-day woman with compassion and valor, and grace."

Marney beamed, shaking his hand with relief. "Hannah is where she needs to be right now, helping those students and their families—along with the nation," she said.

"That's for sure," Bumpy smiled. "She's America's guardian angel!"

"That she is, Mr. Friedman . . . that she is!"

Marney looked over into the glass conference room and smiled. It would be a stunning cast, indeed. The women of *The Gab* were as fierce and beautiful as they come. She knew that no truer words had ever been spoken, and for Hannah, it was just the beginning.

~End~

ABOUT THE AUTHOR
★ ★ ★

JAMIE COLLINS, AUTHOR OF THE "Secrets and Stilettos" series, writes larger than life fiction about the fast-track world of media and entertainment.

As a former model/actress, she infuses her stories with Hollywood grit, sizzle and heat reminiscent of the great women's fiction writers (Jackie Collins, Sidney Sheldon, and Olivia Goldsmith) of decades past on which she cut her writing chops reading and emulating their iconic styles.

Collins brings a fresh, modern-day take on the throwback pocket novel tomes that defined an era of extravagance and excess in exchange for a world where women are more powerful, smart, and driven than ever.

Collins's stilettos have been everywhere from nightclubs in Japan, to the Playboy mansion, to dinner with a Sinatra. Her aim is to delight and entertain readers of women's fiction everywhere.

Visit Jamie Collins's website where you can join her reader list and get started with a **free** copy of the prequel to the series, *Sign On!*

Link: *www.jamiecollinsauthor.com*

Then jump right in, starting with, *Blonde Up!* The first book in the four-part "Secrets and Stilettos" series—a behind the scenes look at the competitive, glamorous, and often exploitative world of media and entertainment—available now at your favorite eBook retailer. Look for *Sexy Ink!*—book four coming out in early 2019.

Follow Jamie Collins on Twitter.

Visit Jamie Collins on Facebook.

Check out Jamie Collins's feed on Instagram.

Head over to Jamie's website for contact and other information at: *www.jamiecollinsauthor.com*

BOOKS BY JAMIE COLLINS:

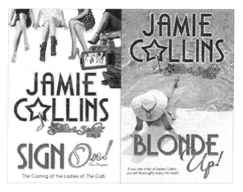

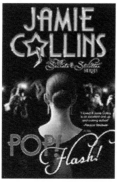

Made in the USA
Middletown, DE
08 January 2021

31110853R00168